Into SOMNIARE

AVA WIXX

First Edition: September 2024
Published in the United States of America by
Wicked Wixx Press.
The Wicked Wixx Press Logo is a trademark of
Wicked Wixx Press.
Originally published under the title
Somniare: March 2016

Cover Art, Ava Wixx Logo, Wicked Wixx Logo, & Interior Book
Graphics by Lindsay Tiry of LT Arts
Illustrations by J.N. Sheats
Edited by Melissa Ringsted of There For You Editing

Print ISBN: 978-1-955950-36-7
Kindle ISBN: 978-1-955950-37-4
EPUB ISBN: 978-1-955950-38-1

For more information visit: avawixx.com

All that we see or seem
is but a dream within a dream.
~*Edgar Allan Poe*

SHE DREAMT A LITTLE DREAM
ESCAPING A BRUTALITY
BUT NOTHING IS WHAT IT SEEMS
WHEN STEPPING OUT OF REALITY ...

Chapter 1

I'd always thought my life would end with a roar— me waging battle with death itself.

It didn't happen that way.

One moment I was alive—vibrant—on the verge of greatness. And then it all slipped away … silently, like whispered words of regret on the wind.

Or maybe I simply didn't remember parts of my murder. That was a distinct possibility.

Now in Somniare, hanging onto quasi-life by a thread, one-by-one my memories were being siphoned from my mind … and there was nothing I could do about it.

I grunted with displeasure as I fell on my ass, more annoyed than afraid. "Go away! Die! Be vanquished already!"

Hovering a few feet above me, nothing but a dark shadowy mass, was a larua. This particularly nasty kind was one indigenous to Somniare. It targeted beings that didn't belong in the dreaming landscape, like me, sucking away one memory from my life at a time.

I shuddered when I thought about what would happen if I lost everything. I'd become one of them—a larua. I'd have no emotions, and no memories of my own, so I'd crave those things, stealing them from others whenever I could.

I screamed as dark tentacles swirled towards me, fear finally taking hold, freezing me in place. Once I could have stopped it with a simple command or motion. *Magic.* My magic threaded by intent through my words or actions would have enforced my will over the larua, but not now. No, now I was weak, my magic used up to keep me in Somniare until I could find a way out. If I let my resolve waver for even a moment, using any energy to ward off the larua, there was a chance I'd be dead for good.

"Just go away," I gritted out, squeezing my eyes shut. I despised how helpless I felt. Nothing—and I do mean *nothing*—makes you feel more powerless than knowing you can't fight something.

Warmth washed over me; pleasant, almost reassuring, and completely at odds with what was about to happen to me. My breath hitched as I waited to see what memory I would experience before it was lost to me forever.

"Leave her alone!" a deep voice rumbled, seemingly from all around me.

Frost filled my lungs and I gasped for air, clawing at my chest. I was held in pitch-blackness, unable to see anything. My thoughts were scattered, and unfocused. The larua had touched me, that much I was sure of, but … but was it still? *What's happening?*

"I said, you need to be leavin' her alone! Now!"

Bright colors exploded into existence, chasing away the darkness with ferocity. My heart thrashed against my ribcage as my lungs fully expanded with oxygen. I fell onto my back, staring at—

"Hey. You alright?"

A slow smile curled my lips upward, even as I struggled to regain my composure. An astoundingly attractive male was peering down at me, his baby blues filled with concern.

Why, hello there. Aren't you just cute enough to die for me?

I offered my hand to the dashing stranger, grinning widely as I got a better look at him. He appeared to be in his early to mid-twenties, his face a study in masculinity, all hard lines and sharp angles. Dark blond scruff shaded his jaw, matching his short-cropped hair. Wearing nothing but a T-shirt and military-style fatigues, his muscular body was on display for me to drink in.

Oh, yes, he's definitely what I need.

I'd been beginning to fear never finding a human, let alone one up to my standards, who I could use to get me the hell out of Somniare. *Call me picky.* After all, in the end, the human would end up dead, so it shouldn't have mattered, but it did to me. If I was going to bond with someone on any level, I wanted it to be enjoyable.

I frowned when the male backed up a few steps,

careful not to touch me. My hand hung limply in the air for a second before I let it drop into my lap. *How embarrassing.*

A soft shimmer wavered around him, and then a bright flash of pink caused me to turn my head for a moment. When I looked back, a little girl stood in his place, smiling at me mischievously.

"Hey! Where did he …" Realization kicked in. I narrowed my eyes. "What are you?" *I so don't have time for this—so much for my ticket out of Somniare.* Disappointment nettled me.

The girl fluffed her shoulder-length white hair, studying me with odd pink-tinged eyes. Her features were sharp, lupine somehow. "I'm your hero." She tilted her head to look down at her body. "Or I guess heroine now." She giggled, the sound tinkling through the air.

I staggered to my feet, pushing my annoyance aside. After all, the—whatever it was—had saved me from the larua. "Thank—" I swallowed my words, internally chastising myself for the near slip-up. One should never thank a creature of unknown origins. Some seemingly simple words hold more power than most fathom. I wasn't about to risk owing a debt that could put me in a worse situation than I was already in, however slim the chance. "Your assistance was greatly appreciated." I forced a smile. "Now get lost." I didn't need the complication of a new friend.

The girl's delicate hands shifted to her hips. "I don't think so, Aremidalia Novem, next Grand Witch of Domus

Novem. You're not getting rid of me that easily. In fact, you're kind of stuck with me."

"Oooh, no. I made no deal with you to save me. Nor did I offer my gratitude in the form of those two little seemingly innocuous words. I think we both know which ones I'm talking about. What you just did, that was a freebie." I hated creatures that tried to gain access to my magic by doing favors I didn't ask for and then demanded payment. That wasn't how things worked with witches. If a deal wasn't brokered prior to services rendered, it's what I liked to call a freebie.

She laughed. "I don't think you're understanding me." The air around her shimmered again, and then a flash of purple light blinded me. In the girl's place was a large white fox, with lavender eyes instead of pink. It swished its three tails demonstratively.

I swore under my breath, and muttered to myself, "A damn kitsune. I should have known." *At least it's a young one.* Kitsune's were annoying Japanese foxlike trickster spirits. Annoying because they were powerful, and they liked to get their kicks from causing trouble. You could tell one's age and power level by the number of tails. Luckily, this one only had three.

"Hey! I'm not young! I just got my," it paused, eyeing its fluffy tails, scowling, "third tail!" The fox's voice was multi-layered, sounding weirdly neither masculine nor feminine, unlike when it was in male or female human form.

Had I said the part about it being young out loud? I

scrunched up my nose and crossed my arms over my chest, fighting the urge to roll my eyes. "Exactly. *Only* your third tail. Much appreciation for saving my life ... or memories of it anyways. Bye-bye now." I wiggled my fingers at it before spinning on my heel to walk in the opposite direction.

The fox was suddenly in front of me, its lavender eyes narrowed in frustration. "You don't seem to get it! I'm your familiar! You can't just get rid of me! I came here specifically for you!"

I paused mid-step, trepidation swirling in my gut. "No, huh-uh, nope. Most witches get their familiars when they first come into their powers, which would have been *years* ago for me. Don't screw with me, you little troublemaker."

The kitsune's tails swished rapidly back and forth. "Familiars pick their witches, as you well know, and honey, no one was exactly lining up to be yours."

"What are you trying to say?" I knew I was ... morally ambiguous on my best days. After all, I was raised in Domus Novem. And I definitely was a Novem through and through, but undesirable to a familiar? I was already the most powerful witch in my house, and I hadn't even ascended yet. Familiars were attracted to power, weren't they? I'd thought I hadn't been chosen because I didn't need a familiar. *Talk about a blow to the ego.*

"Just get over yourself already. I picked you, and now you're mine." A flash of blue caused me to blink rapidly, spots dancing in front of my eyes. A young boy stood in the fox's place, grinning.

I groaned, sensing the truth. Of course I'd end up with a damn kitsune for a familiar. *Like my life—or quasi-life—isn't complicated enough as it is.* "So you came here to Somniare to help me?" I jiggled my foot, resisting the urge to tap it against the ground. "Where've you been? It's been—"

"Five minutes since you were murdered. I got here as fast as I could."

I kept my face passive, even though shock rocked my system. *Five minutes?* I would have guessed weeks, if not months. "Five minutes too long. You should have helped prevent my … partial death. Now I have to find a human to get me out of here. But I'm sure you already know that."

The boy was replaced by the fox again. "Laruas usually don't attack so quickly, as you well know. Someone sent them after you. Probably the same someone who murdered you … probably someone close to you. Who knows that you have the ability to send yourself here?"

The only ones who knew my secret were— *No. No, no, no, no, no. Not possible.* I shook my head in denial. "There's no way a Novem would've harmed me. It was the eve of my ascension ceremony. I was to lead them all."

Bitterness formed a lump in my throat. I'd been applying my makeup; vibrant colors adorned my face, concentrated around my eyes with dark smoky shadow and liner, along with a spectacular blood-red lipstick, which I did on a whim. Masks and full makeup were expected at an ascension ceremony. It was meant to be a celebration—a grand party for the new Novem Grand

Witch, kind of like Halloween meets Mardi Gras, but with actual magic. I'd even taken the time to curl my normally straight sable locks into a cascading mane that many would have envied. I remembered admiring myself before … before it all slipped away.

"Oh come on, Novems aren't exactly known for being lux witches. You—"

"Like to play in the grey. We're neither lux (light) witches nor tenebris (dark) witches. We mind our own damn business and sell our spells. No one gets hurt." *Mostly.*

The kitsune tilted its head, and I was pretty sure if it was in human form its eyebrows would have been raised in vivid skepticism. "You sell your spells to morally corrupt people who use them to—"

"Hey! If they've got cash, what do I care what they do with our spells? It's not like we sell black magic spells and trinkets, and I happen to like nice things. None of that means a Novem would murder their future leader hours before she—*I* took over the house. We're loyal to each other."

"Then explain the laruas, and how easily someone had access to you."

Silence fell over us as I mulled over the kitsune's argument. I hated to admit it, but it did kind of have a point. "But why?"

"Power?"

"Domus Novem doesn't care about power like that. Not like some of the other domos."

My mind wandered briefly to the other eight houses of magic, or domos magicae. Three were lux domos, three tenebris domos, and two grey domos, like mine, which technically wasn't a thing in magic, and was why we were mostly ignored. The lux and tenebris domos were always battling, and neither group bothered to so much as look down their noses at us hiding out in the grey areas of the moral compass. But still ...

It was definitely too much of a coincidence that I'd been murdered mere hours before I would have ascended into my full powers and taken my position as Grand Witch. And I had been talking about making some changes—changes that could have garnered a bit of attention from some of the other domos. Attention I hadn't counted on possibly getting. I wanted to make things good for everyone in Domus Novem. After all, what was the point of power if it had no purpose? Things can't improve if change isn't allowed to happen. But what if some of the other domos didn't want change? What if they saw change in Domus Novem as threatening?

Or, maybe someone I'd mistakenly trusted had murdered me. There might have been a few witches in Domus Novem who resented me ascending at such a young age. I didn't make the rules, though, the magic did. It had domain over all of us when you got down to it. It wasn't like I wanted to be Grand Witch and assume the mantle of responsibility before I really got to experience life. I would have been happy to wait, say another fifty years or so, but I didn't get a choice.

"I just think you need to consider the possibility that—"

"Look, whatever your name is, I don't exactly trust you. You just show up here—"

"Run!"

My eyes widened as I processed what was approaching, what could only be described as an angry mass of chaos—a horde of laruas. Utterly petrified, my mind blanked. Luckily, adrenaline vibrated through my system, propelling me into motion. I tore off into the eerie forest, which hadn't been quite so creepy a few moments ago, but now was illuminated by a pale blue cast. Branches grabbed at me, tearing at my face and body. The pain of my multi-tree assault barely registered as I pressed on, not daring to look behind me.

"Hurry! Hurry! Hurry!" the kitsune yelled as it dashed in front of me, weaving back and forth, tails whirling in a circle.

"Can't you scare them off like the other—"

"No! Too many!"

In front of me, a few feet away, a large masculine form stepped out from behind a tree. His body was encased almost completely in black leather, and topped with a heavy hood that obscured his face from my view entirely. I skidded to a stop, tumbling face first, getting a mouthful of dried leaves. Sputtering, I scrambled forward, my clothes limiting my mobility. *Goddamn dress! Why the hell did I have to be murdered in this thing?*

"Stay down," a gravelly, baritone voice commanded. A

large foot was placed on the middle of my back, like I was a footstool, forcing me to obey. I opened my mouth to protest, my pride overriding all fear, but I was silenced by something akin to a sonic boom.

My ears still ringing, I dazedly rolled onto my back when the foot was removed. I blinked, focusing on the hooded figure looming over me. "What the hell is your problem?" I lifted my hand, palm out, wishing I could blast him with my magic. Of course, if I could have spared the energy, I wouldn't have been on the run to begin with.

"You're welcome."

I wasn't even sure what he'd done. I hadn't actually *seen* anything. Ignoring him, I lurched to my feet, darting my gaze to where the laruas had been a few moments ago. They were gone. I heaved a sigh of relief, straightened my long skirt, and started walking.

"A thank you might be nice."

I paused, not bothering to glance back at my supposed savior. *Ha! Not happening! I may be young, but I wasn't born yesterday.* I knew without getting a glimpse beneath his dark hood what I'd see. He would be beautiful, devastatingly so, with features almost too perfect. His eyes would be jewel-toned, cruel and hard, and his ears would swoop up into the smallest of points. His power hummed along my skin, familiar, letting me know exactly what he was. *Fae.* I was generally paranoid about thanking anyone, but one should *never* thank a fae under *any* circumstances. You'd end up owing things you might not ever be able to pay—or worse—you would. "Yeah, it would be nice, wouldn't it? But those words aren't passing my lips ... ever. At least not directed at you."

He chuckled, long and low. "I see, *cailleach*." The faint lilt to his voice somehow managed to be beautiful, despite the words. It was distinctly fae—almost Irish, yet not, a bit Scottish, but not as rough. The cadence was musical and yet primal at the same time. *Stupid fae. Even their accents are hard to pin down.*

I ground my teeth together. I'd attempted to ignore the word that meant hag but failed horribly. *Cailleach, really?* It's what the fae favored calling any female witch, no matter her age or appearance. The term was an insult, although I didn't completely understand it. Sure, witches weren't immortal like the fae, and we did eventually age, unless we dabbled in black magic, but we were incredibly long-lived and didn't turn decrepit until at least a handful of centuries passed. Obviously, I didn't get the fae sense of humor. All I knew was that I had just turned seventeen years old, and there was nothing haggy about me, therefore the whole thing pissed me off.

"Do you *see?* Do you *really?*" I whirled around to face him, but he was gone. I kicked a pile of leaves, wishing it was the fae's face. Witches and fae didn't get along. We weren't enemies, exactly, but there was history there— history of both races trying to screw the other over. To say I didn't trust their vile species was the understatement of the year. *Why did he save me? What's his angle?* Because there was always an angle with a fae.

My negligent familiar popped into existence at my feet in fox form, its tails twitching excitedly. "That was close."

Narrowing my eyes, I tapped my foot. "Yeah, it was. Thanks for being ever so helpful."

I tugged at my skirt, wishing for a wardrobe change. It was like being stuck at a costume party for too long. While the gown had seemed fun at first, and I'd been so excited to don the magnificent blue creation made just for me, I wanted nothing more than to be in an old, worn pair of jeans and some shit-kickers. *Note to self: Never wear a dress again. One never knows when one could end up semi-dead and stuck in the monstrosity way past its expiration date.*

"You probably shouldn't antagonize Kiernan, by the way. He—"

"What? That arrogant fae who just tried to get me to thank him?"

"One and the same. It's probably a good idea if you—"

"He called me a *hag*. Did you hear him?" I kicked the ground, muttering, "Stupid asshat."

Male fae were the worst. They thought that any female from any species should bow down at their feet. The real problem was, with their beauty and powers, most did.

"You're kind of missing the point here, Remy."

"Oh, we're on casual terms now? No more Aremidalia, huh? I guess I missed the part where we became actual friends." I lifted my gaze to study the kitsune. It was still in fox form, and I found myself wondering if my new life-long companion was male or female. With a creature like a kitsune, there was no way to tell, at least that I was privy to. "What are you anyways? A boy or a girl?"

It lifted its head and sniffed. "You play in the grey, well so do I."

I quirked an eyebrow. "And what exactly does that mean?"

"It means you're *morally* ambiguous ... and I'm *gender* ambiguous. I neither identify as male or female. I'm both."

Had I said the part about me being morally ambiguous out loud? Or was the kitsune already reading my mind? It usually took a lot longer for that kind of connection to form between a witch and their familiar. I shrugged, realizing I didn't really care about any of it. It was what it was. "Yeah, okay. I just wanted to know before I named you. Finding a cool gender-neutral name may be a toughie though." I tapped my chin and stared at the kitsune.

"You could just let me name myself. You know, since I already have one and all." Hope danced in my familiar's eyes.

"Nope. I get stuck with a kitsune, I'm naming it." I smirked. "Besides, I missed out on so many other bonding experiences with you, wouldn't want to go against tradition on this, too. Now let me think ..." I continued to study the foxlike trickster. The name would have to be gender-neutral and yet something cool. Even though I kind of wanted to antagonize the kitsune for some elusive reason, I also knew it would be associated with me for life, so I didn't want something too crazy like Foxface, or Fluffy.

"Just hurry up and name me already before we get attacked by more laruas."

Grinning, I snapped my fingers. "I got it! Unagi!"

"What?" A bright blue light flashed, and a huge, angry male—who kind of resembled a lumberjack—glared down at me. "You want to name me after freshwater eel? Do I look like sushi to you? What the hell is wrong with you?"

I raised my hands in the air, backing up a few steps. "I thought it was some kind of Japanese fighting style, I swear. But it still sounds cool." *Lie.* I knew exactly what I was doing. Laughter bubbled up and burst from my chest as I started walking. "Yep, I think I'm going to stick with it. Unagi it is."

"I can't go by Unagi," it whined. "I just can't."

"It's your new name, get used to it."

"And you wonder why no familiar wants you besides me." Bright purple light flashed, revealing the fox once more.

I rolled my eyes. "Please." I picked up the pace, heading deeper into the forest. Unagi lagged behind as if each step was painful with its new name.

I had an almost unending list of questions that I wanted to pepper my familiar with. The first of which would be: where did it get all of its information about me? I opened my mouth to start what would certainly turn into an interrogation when the air filled with a desperate wail from a child. The piteous sound reached into my chest and squeezed, causing me to stumble. Once I righted myself, I turned in the direction it had come from and took off at a dead sprint.

I may be a bit of a mercenary, but I'm not heartless. If a child needed help, I would do what I could. I didn't pause to contemplate where I was or the consequences of my actions. Nor did I care if Unagi followed me.

I had one thing on my mind.

Get to the child.

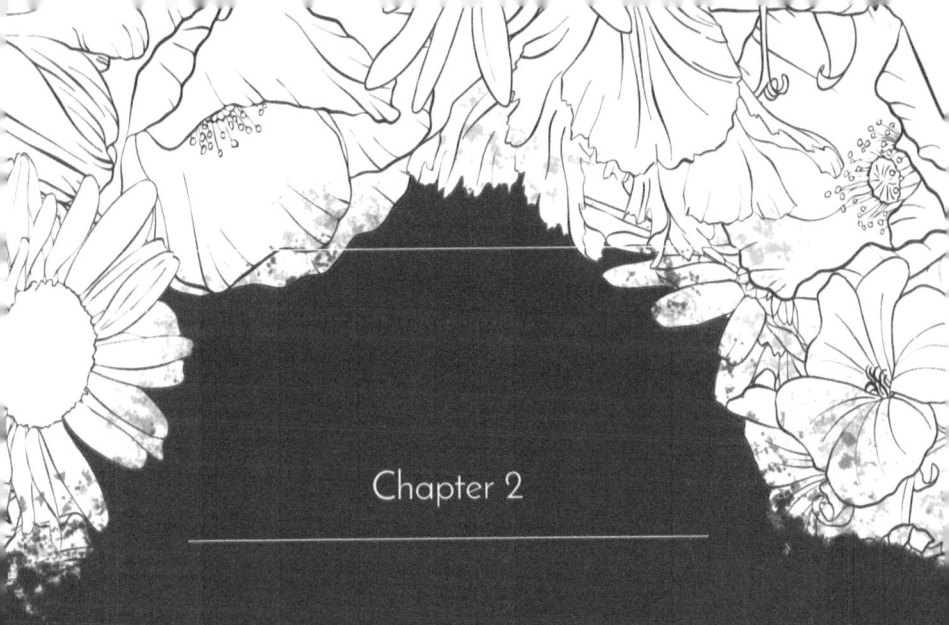

Chapter 2

I'd had it drummed into my head since birth that a witch should trust her intuition. We're attuned to things beyond general comprehension, and therefore limiting ourselves to the parameters set by basic logic is just plain stupid. Magical intuition trumps logic every time. I'd never questioned the notion, believing what I'd been taught wholeheartedly, right up until the moment I laid eyes on the child I'd been driven to find ... and help.

Blood. There was blood everywhere. The macabre scene left me reeling, and the smell—the stale odor of dried leaves mixed with decay was ... rancid. I nearly gagged. A small child, a baby really, sat amid the gore, limbs, and various body parts decorating the ground around it. The thing—I could no longer think of it as a child, more like a creature, or a child-shaped monster—turned its attention to me when a small, involuntary squeak escaped my throat. It opened its mouth to wail, and the minute the forlorn note reached my ears, I was caught in its thrall again. Part of my mind recognized what was happening, and why I'd set off to help the thing before I'd considered ... well, anything, but I couldn't stop myself from being drawn to it.

With one shaky step after another, I inched closer to the creature, its luminous eyes taking me in hungrily. I inhaled deeply, trying to center myself, but the copper tang of blood caught in my throat, curdling my stomach instead. *Stop. Stop. Stop. Stop going towards the thing. Move away! Move away now! You're about to be its next meal.* I internally shuddered, thoughts of my limbs strewn about with the others assaulting my mind. The thing looked so innocent, fat fists reaching for me like it simply wanted a hug, not to eat my face off.

This isn't your dream. It has no power over you. It has no power over you. And yet ... it seemed to have power over me. It didn't make sense. In theory, the only things that should have been able to harm me in Somniare were the laruas, and other visitors that didn't belong. The rest should have been background noise to me, but ... the trees. I lifted a shaky hand to trace the scratches on my face. Those shouldn't have hurt me either. *What the hell is going on?*

"Looks like you need my help again, *cailleach.* I wonder, would you thank me this time?"

"Hell no, I wouldn't," I growled, my teeth clenched so

tight my jaw ached. "I'd rather be a mid-day snack for this thing than owe you anything."

Kiernan laughed. "I don't think you mean that."

"I do. Besides, I can handle this myself. No help necessary." The creature licked its lips as I drew another scant inch closer to its deadly grasp.

"Yes, it looks like you have everything well under control." I could hear the smirk in his voice.

If I get out of this mess in one piece, I'm seriously going to punch him right in his smug fae face, consequences be damned.

I closed my eyes, searching for my inner strength. Sweat formed on my upper lip and forehead, spilling down my face. I didn't need magic to resist a dream terror conjured up by some human. *The cannibal child-creature has no power over me. I'm stronger than it, and this place. I can resist its call. I will prevail—without some smug fae's help.*

My entire body shook with the force it took to resist the next step forward, sweat dribbling down my spine. The creature's wail grew louder in response. My foot hovered mid-step, my balance wavering as I attempted to pull back. My eyes flew open as I teetered precariously, my arms flailing wildly. *I can't fall. I won't. The little monster will be close enough to sink its teeth into me if I do.*

"I really think you should take his help," Unagi snapped from behind me.

"What about you? Can't you—"

"Just take his help!"

"No!"

I lurched forward, my arms pinwheeling in an attempt

to stop the inevitable. My gaze locked onto the now silent creature as it reached for me, its bloodied lips stretching into a smile, exposing razor-sharp teeth.

And then I was airborne, flung back from the monster, landing with an *oof* on my ass. The creature shrieked with rage as I gazed up into the shadow of Kiernan's hood. "Is not thanking me worth your life?" Tension radiated from him in palpable waves.

"I would have figured something out," I muttered, glancing at my muddied and torn skirt.

He jerked me off the ground by my shoulders, shaking me roughly. "This isn't a game. It would have torn you to pieces in a matter of seconds."

I lifted my chin defiantly. "Stop manhandling me. I may not be able to use my powers right now, but you'll be sorry when I get out of here." He let me go like my skin had burned his fingers. I stumbled, somehow managing to stay standing.

"Stupid, *cailleach*. I thought you were different, but I can see now that you're all the same." Kiernan disappeared right in front of my eyes. One minute he was there, and the next ... *poof*, gone.

His words rankled me. Not just the whole hag thing again, but the rest, too. All witches weren't the same. *Dumbass*. But I didn't have time to worry about the slight from Kiernan.

I spun around, my gaze landing on the child-like creature again. It gnashed its razor teeth at me, angry eyes riveted, but the wail that filled the air was no longer a problem for me. The spell had been broken, so to speak. "Ha! Nice try, little cannibal baby! You're going to have to find your next meal somewhere else!" Unable to resist, I stuck my tongue out.

"Mature," Unagi said, its fox face staring at me with disapproval. "You do realize that the little cannibal baby is just someone's dream—or nightmare. It isn't sentient in the way that—"

"Whatever." I pivoted on my heel, heading into the woods away from the bloodthirsty baby. "I need to get the hell out of here before I lose my mind. What I need is to find one of the human dreamers, not what their subconscious conjured up."

The problem was, I didn't know how to find one. It wasn't like they were stumbling around Somniare ... like me. All the times I'd visited the dreamscape before, I'd done so for fun, learning what I could about the land. Dreamers were definitely more prevalent then. It was as if they sensed the danger I was to them now. Of course, there was always the possibility that I had known how to find a dreamer, and a larua had sucked away that knowledge ... which would be eerily convenient. Or planned. My gut twisted with anxiety. What if—

I gasped, my lungs constricting, not even having time to scream. My body somersaulted, end over end, falling through the air. I widened my eyes, trying to make sense of what I was seeing. Clocks of every type and size whizzed past me as I plummeted through the center of the tunnel containing them. Grabbing wildly at anything within my reach, my fingers slid helplessly from every surface as I continued to fall.

"Remy!" I recognized Unagi's multi-layered fox voice, and I kicked my arms and legs out so I was free-falling with my face up, my dark hair whipping into my eyes. Above me, Unagi flew through the air, its three tails whirling furiously. "Grab onto me!"

I stretched my arms, reaching, straining to get to Unagi. But my hands continued to touch only air.

Suddenly, I slammed into the ground, everything disappearing. I lay there for a moment, half expecting Unagi's furry body to land on mine, but all remained silent and dark. I lurched to my feet, disoriented, but pain free.

"Hello!" I called. "Unagi?" I tilted my head to listen but got no response. "Anyone?"

"Remy, what are you doing?" my older sister's soft voice echoed through the void.

"Callie?" My heart leapt into my throat.

"Remy, give me that."

I bit my lip, disappointment coursing through my system. It turned out I was still alone after all. *Of course I am, there's no way Callie could possibly be here.*

An image flickered a few feet in front of me, as if being played from an old-school projector. It was a scene from my childhood. I fell into the memory.

"Why, Callie?" I clutched the stuffed voodoo doll in my arms. I'd labored for hours over it, my small fingers sore and bleeding from my efforts. "Is something wrong?"

"Just give me the doll, Remy."

I clutched it tighter, shaking my head. "I made it all by myself. I wanted to use her for—"

My sister snatched the doll from me with ease; my small arms no match for her. "Callie!" I snapped, indignant. "That's mine, give it back. Now."

Her expression softened as she studied my face and then the doll. "Remy, baby, why did you give it a smile ... and a heart?"

I shrugged, suddenly embarrassed. But I knew my sister wouldn't let it go until she got an answer. She'd always been more like a second mother to me than an older sibling. "I wanted to practice doing love spells."

She laughed. "Love spells? With a voodoo doll? Remy, baby, that's not what a voodoo doll is for. And Novems don't do love spells."

My lower lip quivered, my cheeks heating with shame. I hated feeling stupid. "What's a voodoo doll for then? And why don't we do love spells?"

Ignoring my questions, my sister handed me back the doll. "Here. You can keep it, as long as you don't practice magic on it. Especially love spells." Her gaze slid over the doll once more, her lips twitching. "It's kind of cute, but don't tell anyone I said that."

"I don't want it anymore." I hurled the doll at the ground, tears dripping from my lashes.

The scene ended abruptly, throwing me into darkness again. I could smell the lingering scent of my sister's flowery body-spray. I choked back a sob. That day was the last time I'd seen Callie alive. I'd been only five years old.

After her tragic death, I'd searched for that stupid doll, wanting it because I thought I would feel close to her somehow, but I never found it.

Exhaustion tugged at me, and I flopped onto my back, cold ground coming up to meet me. *Maybe I just need a little nap.* I yawned, turning onto my side and curling up in a little ball. I used my arm as a pillow, my eyes fluttering shut.

Wait, what happens when you fall asleep in Somniare?

All went dark.

Chapter 3

"I dreamt I was a butterfly, and upon awakening, I didn't know if I was the man dreaming I was the butterfly, or the butterfly dreaming the man."

"What's that supposed to mean?" I couldn't open my eyes; it was as if they were glued shut. "Is that you, Unagi?"

Sweat pebbled on my upper lip, and with a grunt, I managed to get my eyes open, my lashes peeling apart reluctantly. I swayed, coming to the realization that I'd somehow been standing the entire time. My gaze tracked down to my sister's lifeless body lying crumpled at my feet, her expression vacant and dull. In her arms was my voodoo doll. I dropped to my knees, soundless sobs escaping my chest.

"You can save her." The words slithered around me, seducing my will.

"I don't know how to do that kind of magic. I'm not a necromancer."

"You know how."

Yes. I do know how. It would be easy. So easy.

I lifted my hands to hover over my sister's chest. "Live," I demanded, my magic infusing with my words. "Live!"

My vision wavered, black spots dancing in front of my eyes. *Wait. Somniare. I was murdered. This can't be real. Something's trying to get me to waste my energy.* I yanked my hands away, screaming with the effort it took to recall my magic into my body. The energy slammed back into me, throwing me, and I sailed through the air, landing in a heap.

"Nooooo!" a masculine voice roared, capturing my attention.

I clawed the ground, managing to get to my feet. Behind me was what appeared to be a wall of mirrors. It was now the only source of light. Curious, I rushed to the glass, realizing it was a window, and pressed my hands and face against it in an attempt to see what was on the other side.

"Noooo!" the same masculine voice roared again.

Dark, eerie fog rolled away from the window to reveal a boy, no older than thirteen, battling a shadowy figure in a desert terrain. Swords clashed as the two moved almost too fast for my eyes to track. Instead, my gaze focused on something else in the scene—a body.

There on the parched ground, was a girl, about the same age as the boy, her lavender eyes staring lifelessly in my direction. Blood pooled around her small form, darkening her long white hair, and staining the once light-colored edges of her clothing. *Wait ... lavender eyes.* They were identical to Unagi's. But how?

I swung my gaze back to the battle that was still waging. The young boy was holding his own, much to my surprise. He wielded a katana, the silver of it glinting in the sun, appearing to glow. His white hair was plastered to his face with sweat, as was his clothing, some kind of kimono, black with white edging.

Rage, sorrow, confusion ... all rolled through me, but I knew they weren't my emotions. *Unagi. They have to be coming from Unagi. Our bond is strengthening.*

I pounded against the window. "Unagi! Can you hear me? Unagi!"

I didn't know exactly what I was seeing, but I had a pretty good idea that it was some kind of twisted memory like I'd been subjected to. Somehow I'd been able to get myself out of mine, but I wasn't so sure Unagi had that power.

The shadowy figure lunged, his sword sinking into the boy's chest. He pulled the sword out, took a few steps back, and disappeared. The boy collapsed onto the ground, his eyes meeting mine, his form shifting to match the dead girl's body.

"No!" I bellowed, slamming my fists against the glass. I still wasn't sure what I was witnessing, but I knew I had to put a halt to it.

Magic trickled out of my palms, just a bit, but

apparently enough. Shards exploded outward, heat rushing past me as I hunched over in pain, gripping my side. Blood bloomed on the fabric of my dress. *What's happening?*

"Remy!" I found myself cradled in strong arms, a boy not much older than my seventeen years staring down at me, lavender eyes studying and assessing. "You shouldn't have done that."

I trailed bloody fingertips across his lupine face, curiosity overwhelming any fear. "Is this you?"

He was absolutely stunning. Long white hair skimmed his shoulders, braids holding it back from his face at the temples. His angular jaw was sharp, with no scruff marring the utter perfection. He was almost androgynous, but had just a tad too much masculinity to be quite defined that way, or maybe it was simply because he was young, not fully matured yet. I was completely mesmerized. I'd never seen anyone, or anything, not even fae, as beautiful as him. A familiar longing threatened to overwhelm me, and yet I wasn't sure why.

His eyes widened, some unknown emotion rolling like storm clouds across his features, darkening his visage. I attempted to delve into his mind, but found it closed off.

"No." The clipped response felt like a slap, and I cringed.

Purple flashed and a girl replaced the boy, just as beautiful in her own way, with the same long white hair framing angular features. "I told you, I'm neither male nor female. I'm both."

She pressed her lips to mine, stealing all coherent thought. Magic rushed into my system, the spicy flavor sliding down my throat and energizing me. Before I had the chance to react, the kiss ended, and I found myself on the ground, alone. My mind spun, images of things progressing much further than they actually did dancing across my brain. The thing was, I didn't know if I wanted the boy or the girl. *Maybe both.* I bit my lip, lost in the fantasy.

"I'm your familiar. You shouldn't have thoughts— thoughts like that about me." Unagi, back in fox form, sat a few feet away, tails twitching back and forth, back and forth.

Shame heated my cheeks. It wasn't that I was thinking of being with a guy … and a girl. I wasn't embarrassed that I was attracted to both sexes, even though I lacked experience with either. It was the fact that Unagi was right, he—she—it was my familiar. Some things were just wrong, and having any kind of sexual thoughts about a familiar definitely fell under that category. The bond between a witch and his or her familiar was profound, and it went much deeper than anything sexual. I was cheapening everything with my immaturity. I'd trained for a lot of things, but never this.

"I'm sorry. I didn't mean— I just— My hormones have a mind of their own. Not an excuse, but I-I can't—" I clamped my mouth shut and glared at my bloody hands.

"It's fine. Just don't—"

"Let's just pretend it didn't happen. Thanks for replenishing my magic. That was a close one."

"Don't do something like that again. I don't have much magic to spare. Luckily, you didn't lose more than I had to give."

"I was dying—all the way." I gulped, the reality of what nearly happened finally catching up with me. I wanted to believe I'd been focusing on sexual fantasies as a way of avoiding the reality of my near-permanent death. I wasn't so sure it was the truth, though. It saddened me on some level that I could die without ever having experienced that part of life; love, sex, a real relationship with intimacy. I always thought I'd have time to worry about that kind of stuff when I was older, but now I wasn't so confident I'd make it out of Somniare in one piece. *No. Stop it. You're going to be fine. You need to ditch the doom and gloom attitude.*

"But you're not dying now."

"No, not now."

I dropped my gaze to my dress, the blood on it already dry. I didn't want to think any more about how close I'd come to true death. By using the little bit of magic to break the glass, my body had begun to revert to the state it'd been in before I'd escaped to Somniare, the stasis I was maintaining slipping away. I didn't really understand all the logistics of my quasi-life, but that was the thing about magic, you didn't always have to, you just had to know the rules to make it work. Thankfully, those rules hadn't been stolen by the laruas ... yet.

I shook my head in an attempt to clear my mind. *Focus*

on the now—on the present. I stood slowly, nibbling my bottom lip. "Where are we?"

"Mama?"

I squinted at Unagi. "What did you just say?"

"That wasn't me."

"Mama?"

I spun around, searching the dark for the source of the tiny voice. Now that I listened carefully, I realized it sounded like a small child and not Unagi at all. I picked up on some movement and tensed for whatever was coming towards us. *Please don't be another cannibal baby.*

My jaw dropped when I got my first look at what was actually approaching ... A voodoo doll.

My voodoo doll.

It gazed at me with uncertainty, one shiny, button eye gleaming, the other marked only with an X of thread. The small sewn-on smile moved slightly when it spoke, "Mama?" again. Its raggedy arms reached for me as it crept steadily closer, and its blue and purple yarn pigtails swung around its face. I took a step backwards and it stopped moving, its arms dropping limply at its sides. "Mama?"

I brought a shaky hand up to cover my mouth, my gaze darting over to Unagi. "What is it?"

"Just don't touch it."

"B-but—" My heart squeezed as I stared at the doll. I remembered finding the burlap material in my mother's things, along with the felt, stuffing, yarn, button, and thick thread, all that I'd used to painstakingly create the misshapen thing. My mind flashed to the last time I'd seen it—and my sister.

I want my doll.

I dropped to my knees and opened my arms. It scurried to me as fast as its little legs could carry it, its smile stretched wide into something akin to a grin. "Mama!" it cried, leaping at me with joy. The back of my throat burned with emotion as I scooped it up and squeezed it tightly, ignoring the sharp jab of the pins protruding from its body.

"Remy! Put that ... that *thing* down! You don't know what it is or what it's capable of!"

Ignoring Unagi, I cradled the doll in my arms, petting it softly. "You wouldn't hurt me, would you? No, you wouldn't," I cooed.

"No, Mama. I love you," it said, cuddling into me once more.

"See, it's fine."

"It's not fine! It's—"

"I *said* it's fine." I met Unagi's gaze, daring defiance from my familiar. *I'm the boss here.* "It's coming with us. End of story."

Tension filled the air as Unagi stared back at me. A few heartbeats passed before the fox responded, lips curling with anger. "We don't know how it came into being. We don't know what it could do to you. Or us for that matter. It's not the same doll you made as a child, Remy. It's not connected to your sister."

"It is because I say it is." I set the doll on the ground,

focusing on it. "Can you keep up with us on your own?" It seemed pretty agile from what I'd seen so far, but I just wanted to make sure I wasn't going to have to carry it everywhere. I sniggered as I pictured making Unagi give it a ride like a horse. Or maybe actually shift into a horse. *Could it do that?*

The voodoo doll nodded. "Yes, Mama. I can keep up on my own."

Damn. That would have been funny to see Unagi play horse. I cleared my throat, stifling a full-out laugh. "Okay then." I lifted my head to glare at Unagi again. "We need to find a human to get me out of here. That's what we need to concentrate on."

"You won't be able to bring that thing out into the real world with you. Why bother if—"

"We'll cross that bridge when we get to it. For now, we need to figure out a plan. Do you know where exactly we are, besides in Somniare that is?"

"No," Unagi snapped.

"Well, do you know how to get us back to the forest or the main part of Somniare?"

"No."

"So what do we—"

"Mama?" The voodoo doll tugged at my skirt. "I know the way out of this place."

I quirked an eyebrow and glanced at Unagi. "You do, do you? Well, lead the way … Voo-Dolly."

Unagi groaned. "Voo-Dolly? You're seriously awful at

giving names. And I have a really bad feeling about this. This thing is probably leading us into a trap."

Ignoring Unagi, I trailed along after Voo-Dolly. I couldn't help the smile that tugged at my lips. Maybe my sister had somehow sent the doll from the otherworld to help. Stranger things had been known to happen ... at least in the world of magic. For the moment, I refused to believe anything else.

"Come on, Unagi," I called over my shoulder. "Pick up the pace."

Chapter 4

"I don't trust that thing," Unagi muttered, fox head hanging low, eyes trained on Voo-Dolly.

"I know. You've made your opinion painfully clear."

We'd been walking for what felt like hours, but as I'd already discovered, my perception of time was a bit skewed in Somniare. Luckily, since the start of our trek, we hadn't come across any laruas, cannibal babies, or magic potholes, which is what I labeled the thing Unagi and I had fallen into earlier. *Speaking of cannibal babies …*

"Those other body parts, the ones that creature had snacked on … Just a part of the human's dream, right?" I hadn't had time to really consider it before, but now that I did, I wondered how real any of it was. It was different for me. I wasn't a dreamer, but an unwanted guest in the landscape. Dreams didn't generally kill humans, unless black magic was involved.

"Yes, just part of the dream," Unagi muttered, gaze not even flickering from Voo-Dolly, who was leading the way through a colorful valley.

I inhaled deeply, enjoying the aroma of mixed wildflowers. Unlike scented candles and other overpowering scents, nature usually got it right, even in Somniare, apparently. "So how do we actually know that it would have—"

"We don't know anything for sure. It's not normal for non-dreamers to wander around Somniare."

"Then explain how there are so many laruas." I dipped to grab a sunflower, managing to pluck it without stopping.

"I said it wasn't normal, not that it didn't happen."

I lifted the sunflower to my nose, sniffing it gently. "Mmm…"

"Hey! Don't do that! Put me back! Help! Help me!"

My eyes widened with shock the second I realized that it was the sunflower speaking. A panicked little face stared up at me, leaves and petals quaking with fear. "Oh! I'm—"

"Give her back right now!"

I whirled around, faces appearing on several more flowers. The sweet scents I'd been enjoying turned overpowering, pungent almost, the air thickening with pollen.

"Run!" I yelled, dropping the sunflower and making a mad dash across the field. My arms and legs pumping, I ate up the ground, screams of panic and rage surrounding me.

"Murderer!"

"Flower killer!"

"Someone help us!"

"Come back here so we can use your carcass to fertilize our dirt!"

I wanted to kiss the flower-free ground when I reached it, Unagi and Voo-Dolly arriving right behind me.

"How did you know they'd turn … ugly?" Unagi sniffed the air, staring back at the murderous flowers that were still waving and screaming at us.

It was as if there was an invisible wall dividing the land we were now on, and the one we just left. Pollen swirled menacingly around the flower-filled terrain, not touching the one we now stood on. It was bizarre, and very, very welcome in the current situation.

"Please, that dream is recycled. It's been in movies, books … the human who created it isn't very original."

Unagi snorted. "Right."

"Who said a human created it?"

I sighed heavily before turning my gaze upon Kiernan, who was leaning against a tree that hadn't been there a moment ago. His arms and legs were crossed, and his head was tilted down so I couldn't see into his hood. "What now? There's nothing to save me from. I saved myself, so no thanks for you."

"So you did." He chuckled as he shifted his muscular legs. "That won't last long. Creatures such as yourself are a magnet for trouble. You'll need my help again, and I will have your thanks for it."

His original words processed belatedly. "Wait. Did you

create those flowers so you could rescue me? Did you create the cannibal baby and the magic pothole, too?" I whirled around to eye Voo-Dolly. "And the doll? Did you do that?" I was feeling massively set-up.

"Hold on. You're a paranoid little thing, aren't you? I simply meant that humans aren't the only species who dream."

I crossed my arms over my chest, glaring. "Yeah, whatever. Nice attempt at a save. I don't trust you."

"And I don't trust you."

"Why are you even here in Somniare? Huh? You're not a dreamer either." Voo-Dolly sidled up next to me, tugging on my skirt. I glanced down and picked her up, holding her on my hip like a small child. She trembled slightly while staring at Kiernan. "You're scaring Voo-Dolly, go away." I didn't want to believe she was a product of Kiernan's massive set-up. *My sister sent her from the beyond. I know it.*

Pushing off the tree, Kiernan tilted his head, studying Voo-Dolly, and probably my blood-covered dress. "Where did you find that thing? Toss it away. It—"

"I agree with Kiernan," Unagi interjected, who'd been strangely silent since the fae's arrival. "Get rid of that thing before it's too late."

I squeezed Voo-Dolly tighter into me, twining my fingers into one of her pigtails. "Are you two seriously ganging up on me about this?" I glared at Unagi, and hissed, "Traitor. You're my familiar, not his."

"Mama?" Voo-Dolly pressed her face into my arm, voice trembling.

"I'm not throwing her away. Back off. Both of you." I strode into the nearby forest of neon-colored trees, which had appeared a few seconds ago, my head held high. "No one asked you anyways, fae snob."

"Fae snob?" Kiernan's boots crunched the leaves loudly as he followed, grating on my already frayed nerves. "What exactly is a fae snob, pray tell?"

"Why do you care? I'm a witch, and you're fae. We don't have conversations because our kind aren't friends. Ever."

"There was a time when that wasn't true. There was a time when some witches and fae were very … friendly."

"Mmm hmm, until the fae tried to screw the witches over. I know my history."

"History is always skewed by the group telling the story. Don't you think fae are raised to believe the same, but in reverse? Never trust a witch, they're all horrible *cailleaches.*"

I halted, glaring at the arrogant fae. "And you know better, because you were there?"

I could hear the smile when he spoke. "Of course I was."

Curiosity tugged at me, forcing my lips to say the words, "So, what really happened then, Mr. Know-it-all?"

"Let me show you." He lifted his hands, gold light curling from his palms. The swirls of magic wafted lazily through the air, forming a picture in front of us, so real it was like standing in the middle of it. Unagi brushed against my legs, its fox form pressing into me protectively, but not making a move otherwise. I stared, instantaneously riveted.

In the center of a large, ornate bed, lay a couple. The way the female was sprawled across the male's chest, his arm wrapped around her possessively, it was very clear what they must have just been doing.

In the corner of the room, as if one with the shadows, stood a familiar hooded figure. Kiernan. His body was rigid, and his head held high. I couldn't see his face, not that I ever had, but I could tell by his body language that his gaze was not fixated on the couple. His presence struck me as strange, but my attention was quickly diverted when the female spoke.

"Darling," the female murmured, "I have something to tell you."

The male's fingers slid through her long midnight hair lazily. "Yes," he purred. "What is it?"

The tiny rune on the back of my neck burned, clueing me in to the fact that the couple spoke a dialect I wasn't familiar with, but I'd long ago had a language rune etched into my skin. It was a little trick all modern witches used to be able to understand ancient tongues with ease. It required no maintenance and the magic it used fed upon itself, so I wasn't wasting my energy by relying on the rune. It wasn't fail-proof, though, even in the real world, so I was thankful it worked in Somniare at all.

I shifted, trying to get a better look at the couple, but the room was dimly lit, and their features were hard to make out.

All I could tell was that the female was dark in coloring and the male light—like night and day.

"I'm pregnant."

It was as if the world itself held its breath, everything stilling instantly. The male was on his feet the next moment, his nudity slightly jarring. His eyes glowed emerald green, telling me he was fae. "That's not possible if you were taking the potion."

The female pushed herself up onto her elbow, cradling her cheek in her palm, calm despite her partner's distress. "I wanted it. And I shall have it ... we shall have it."

"No," he spat. "It'll be an abomination."

"Abomination?" Her voice rose with ire. "An abomination, you say?"

"Yes. The child cannot be, my love. It just can't."

The female rose, magic crackling in the air audibly. "My love? You dare address me as such when you just called our child an abomination?"

The male's voice softened as he reached for her. "You know it cannot be, you know that the child would—"

"What? What would the child be? Wrong? Because I'm a slave? Or because my magic isn't pure like the fae? Or both? What would make our child such an ... abomination?"

"Darling—"

"Don't darling—my love—any of it!" The female was on the other side of the bed in the blink of an eye, her small frame surrounded by blue flame. "I should have known what this was! I let myself be fooled!" She threw magic at him; the same blue flame that had been harmless to her caused him to cry out in agony as he dropped to the ground, writhing.

Kiernan, who I'd nearly forgotten about, slid from the shadows, moving like a deadly cat. I thought he would come to the male's aid or maybe help the female, I wasn't sure whose side he was on, but instead, he just continued to watch ... but closer. He was waiting for something.

The image scattered as Kiernan's magic blew away, the golden particles hitching a ride on a gust of wind.

"Wait. What? You can't just end it there." I hated to admit it but my curiosity had definitely been piqued. What had Kiernan been doing, and what happened to the couple ... and the baby?

"The rest is too gruesome to show," Kiernan said. "The witch killed her fae lover, but not before he dealt her a blow which put her into a magical coma resulting in her death as well, eventually. And of course, that was the beginning of the end for fae and witch ... relations. Both sides blamed the other, but in truth, two wrongs don't make a right."

"Umm, I only saw one wrong, and it was clearly of fae doing." I absently stroked Voo-Dolly's yarn hair.

Kiernan snorted. "Of course. Why do I keep expecting anything different from you?"

I narrowed my eyes. "What's that supposed to mean? From what I just saw, that guy was diddling a slave, and when he got her pregnant ... well, he acted like a complete jackass."

"All witches were slaves ... in the beginning, as I'm sure you well know. And the king was right, the child would be an abomination."

King? A fae king? Figures. Non-royal fae were bad enough. "How would you know that? And what were you even doing there?" I kicked a pile of leaves, their neon shades somewhat disconcerting.

"I know the child was an abomination because I was there when it was ripped from the witch's womb."

"It lived?" Morbid curiosity caused me to stop short, Unagi running into the back of my legs. "Watch it," I muttered. Unagi merely glared and walked around me, fluttering its tails demonstratively. It seemed oddly like an obscene gesture.

"Yes, it lived. And it was everything the king had feared even though he didn't live to see his son. Fae and witch magic are not meant to be mixed. The child was tainted, and much too powerful. He—"

"It was a boy? And what happened to him?"

"No one knows."

I raised my eyebrows. "Not even you, Mr. Know-it-all?"

"No, not even me."

I could taste the lie on the wind, and yet I knew there was no way I could get the truth out of Kiernan if he didn't want to tell me. "Alrighty then, that was a fun little story." I rolled my eyes.

Something moved into my peripheral vision, and I turned to see what it was. A guy stood by one of the neon trees, one strong arm supporting him as he watched our little group. But it wasn't just any guy, it was one that looked exactly like the hero Unagi had first appeared to me as. I glared down at my familiar. "Want to tell me something?"

"I copy humans I see."

"So he's ..."

"A human dreamer, but he—"

I didn't wait around to hear whatever else Unagi was about to say. I took off across the field, running as fast as I could for the human. "Hey! Hey you! I need to talk to you."

Chapter 5

I was so eager to get out of Somniare, I didn't consider what I'd do if and when I actually caught up to the human. I'd merely seen him ... and went to go get. The fact that I was going to have to seduce his mind, had temporarily escaped mine.

"Hey!" I called again as I got closer. "Please, I need your help."

I was betting on the guy having some kind of hero complex, or at least hoping for one, since he was wearing military-style clothing. *I can play a damsel in distress if I have to.*

He pushed off of the tree and approached me, his stride rigid and efficient as his baby blues traveled over me with concern, taking in my torn and bloody dress, no doubt. He looked exactly as Unagi had represented him. He appeared to be in his early to mid-twenties, his face all hard lines and sharp angles. Dark blond scruff shaded his jaw, matching his short-cropped hair. It was my second time around seeing him, technically, and I thought he was just as gorgeous as my first assessment.

"You hurt?" His voice was even the same deep rumble that Unagi had projected, although I hadn't noticed the southern accent before. It was definitely the icing on the hot guy cake.

So why hadn't Unagi taken me to him? *Me and that kitsune are going to have one serious chat later.*

"No, but—" I glanced over my shoulder at the open field. *Where did everyone go? Shit. Did I drop Voo-Dolly, or had I already set her down? Or maybe Unagi is off ditching her somewhere.* I seethed at the thought and had to force myself to concentrate on the task at hand. "But, um, I need your help getting out of here before I end up dead." Sometimes going with the truth, even partial, is the easiest.

I staggered a bit and feigned being out of breath, panting deeply. A moment later, just as I had desired, the guy took me in his arms without another thought. "Oh yeah, I can definitely help." His lips crashed into mine, his tongue invading my mouth with force. It took me a second to register what was happening.

"Hey!" I yelped, or at least tried to. It was kind of difficult to speak with the guy's tongue halfway down my throat. When his hands started getting a little too friendly, anger heated my blood. *Oh, hell no.*

Magic leapt from my palms into his chest, tossing him a good ten feet up in the air before his body slammed into the ground. I belatedly realized what I'd done. I glanced down to see blood bubbling up from the wound in my side, just as my vision wavered, black pushing in around the edges.

Shit. Why couldn't I have just kicked him in the balls?

I don't wanna die.

$\mathcal{R}$

"REMY!"

My eyes fluttered but didn't quite open. Heat coiled around my body, the scent of wild magic—familiar and welcoming—soothed me, making me want to purr like a cat. "Mmm…" I mumbled.

"I said to back off! You've done more than enough! Remy!"

Slowly it began to register that it was Unagi calling for me in a panicked voice. A part of me cared, worried even, but the rest of me merely wanted to luxuriate in the place of peace I was currently residing in. But then I remembered the field, and the handsy guy—and the blood —me dying … all the way. I sat up, gasping for air, and clutched at my side.

"Calm down." My gaze flicked up to take in Kiernan's hooded figure hovering over me, hands extended. His golden magic swirled from his palms to encase me in some kind of shimmering bubble.

"Remy!" I swiveled on my hands and knees to face in the opposite direction, spotting Unagi and Voo-Dolly in a cage barely big enough to fit both of them. The bars glowed red, letting me know they were magically reinforced.

My entire body tensed, and it took everything in me not to use my magic again. "Why the hell are my familiar and doll in a cage?"

"I needed them out of the way."

"Out of the way for what?"

"Don't listen to him! He snatched us away before you were injured! He—"

I flopped back around and glared up at Kiernan who was still feeding me magic. "He wants my thanks." I knew it with certainty. He'd been after it since I'd first stepped into Somniare.

I nibbled my bottom lip, considering the situation. What kind of powers did Kiernan possess that he could so easily contain a kitsune? Sure, Unagi was still young with only three tails, but powerless my familiar was not. And with that level of skill, why did Kiernan want my thanks so badly? It was time to get some real answers out of the duplicitous fae.

"Tell me why you're so desperate for my thanks. If you have all this magic," I waved my hands in the air, gesturing in a circle, "then why do you need me for anything?"

Kiernan closed his fingers over his palms, the golden glow dissipating slowly along with the bubble I'd been in. I ran my hands over my side, already knowing what I'd find. I was whole again, and my magic had been replenished so I could hold myself in Somniare without aid.

"I have my reasons," Kiernan replied, his gaze fixed on me; I could feel it even if I couldn't see it.

"And you're not going to share?"

His hood moved back and forth slowly. "Not at this time."

I narrowed my eyes, speaking through clenched teeth, "And if I don't give you thanks?"

"You will. Eventually." He turned and left ... the room. Yes, for the first time since waking, I took stock of my new surroundings. I was in a small, barren room, all white —too white, with the cage that held Unagi and Voo-Dolly in the corner. There was nothing else there, not even a window or door.

"What the hell?" I stood, studying the wall where the door had just been, but—

"Forget about it. Apparently, Kiernan has more control in Somniare than I thought."

"Great. Just what I need." I flopped back down, criss-crossing my legs, and rested my elbows on my knees with my chin cradled in my hands. My already torn skirt ripped loudly. I rolled my eyes. "Figures." Not that I really cared. I hated the stupid dress and again wished for pants —any kind of pants at this point—and some kind of comfortable footwear. As it was, my feet were lucky to not be bloody stumps since I'd lost my shoes somewhere along the line.

Unagi's lavender gaze met mine with something akin

to regret. "You might have to thank him and be done with it. I don't see any other way out of this."

"I don't think— Hey, don't do that, Voo-Dolly! You don't know what it could do to you." I grimaced as I watched her pull out one of the pins in her leg and stick it in her arm.

"It doesn't hurt, Mama. They're a part of me, too."

Why did I want the creepy little thing again? Oh, yeah, because Voo-Dolly was connected to my sister somehow. I just knew it … *I think.* I was starting to have my doubts. I decided to contemplate that more later. It wasn't like I could do anything about Voo-Dolly at the moment. Plus, I currently had more pressing matters. "I'm not thanking Kiernan. Can't you turn into an ant or something and squeeze out of there?"

"Sometimes I wonder how much the laruas managed to suck out of your brain before I got to you," Unagi growled, before turning around in the tight space, and flopping down with a harrumph. "Don't you think I already thought of doing something like that? The bars are magically reinforced, as I'm sure you well know, and even if they weren't, I can't change form in here. Again— magically blocked. Maybe if you would have listened to me and hadn't gone running after that human dreamer—"

"You didn't tell me he was some kind of—"

"There were a lot of things I could have told you about him if you would have taken two seconds to listen! There was a reason I didn't take you in search of him! You need to start trusting me!"

Unagi and I glared at each other, both of our chests heaving. Finally, I broke the tension-filled silence. "Fine. Tell me what you know about him now."

Unagi's tails thumped against the ground, which I imagined were spelling out annoyance in Morse code. "Yeah, because that's going to do any good."

I leaned forward, jutting my chin out. "Just tell me. Now. I'm the witch in charge, remember?"

Unagi's tails picked up speed. "Fine."

"Fine."

"All right."

"Just tell me already!" *Damn kitsune.*

"I heard that." Unagi flashed sharp fox teeth.

I crossed my arms over my chest and raised my eyebrows. "Yeah, so?"

"For the love of the gods, you two are giving me a headache!" Kiernan was suddenly behind me, and I fell backwards, my head landing right at his feet. He crouched down, his hands sliding under my shoulder blades.

The next thing I knew, I was in a completely different room. "Hey!" I jerked away from Kiernan, nearly rolling into a piece of furniture. My eyes widened when I realized a large bed dominated the space. I glanced at the bed, then at Kiernan, and then back again. "Oh, hell no! Nope, nope, nope!" I pulled myself to my feet and raised my hands in defense. I'd use my magic, and ultimately kill myself first.

Kiernan stalked closer, one heavy-balled footstep at a time. When he was just out of reach, he stopped, his arms dangling loosely at his sides. "Would it be so bad to be with someone like me? I could guarantee your first time would be pleasurable."

Why do fae accents have to sound so damn sexy? All rumbly and smooth at the same time. God, I haven't even seen his face, what the hell is wrong with my hormones? "I'd rather find pleasure— Wait, ummm... How the hell do you know that I haven't gotten down and dirty yet?" The fact that I was still a card-carrying virgin was definitely not by choice. I'd been forced to spend too much time training as the next Novem Grand Witch, which didn't leave my schedule open for sexual encounters of any kind.

"Down and dirty?" He chuckled. "I know you, Remy. More than you can possibly imagine."

I opened and closed my mouth a few times. "What?"

"People's dreams can reveal a lot about their true selves, and I've been watching yours for some time now." He grabbed my wrists and tugged me into his chest. His voice melted over me, causing me to sway into him. I inhaled deeply. His spicy scent interwoven with leather equaled mouthwatering, and I resisted the urge to bury my nose in his neck. "I'm the one who gave you the ability to send yourself here to begin with. In essence, I saved your life that time, too."

I arched back, trying to put distance between us. "No, that doesn't— It isn't—"

"You recognize the feel of my magic. Don't try and deny it. I've been feeding it to you for some time now." His hands slid down my arms and wrapped around my back.

His wild magic teased my senses, warming my blood, and singing to my soul.

He was right. I did recognize it, and that knowledge was very disconcerting, to say the least. *How the hell didn't I notice before?* I thought back to when I first met him, the familiar hum of his fae magic registering within me, but not once had I looked beyond that to recognize it was … more. I hadn't recognized something more. "But how? How is any of it possible?" So many other questions swirled through my brain but Kiernan didn't give me a chance to ask them. Instead, he released me, much to my surprise.

"Rest. We have much to discuss. I'll be back soon." He disappeared right in front of my eyes, leaving me in a state of utter bewilderment, and a bit of something else that I didn't even want to admit to myself.

I slumped onto the bed, my gaze riveted to the spot Kiernan had just been, his words playing on repeat across my brain.

Rest? Yeah, right.

Chapter 6

O kay, okay, okay …
  Lemme think.
  Just lemme think.
I rubbed my temples. My brain actually ached from the cartwheels it'd been doing. I kept going over the interaction between Kiernan and myself, playing his words over and over in my head, trying to make sense of it … or even the tiniest shred of it, really.

"Would it be so bad to be with someone like me?"

Someone like me? I hadn't considered the word choice earlier, but it was not very fae. Fae were arrogant and egotistical, not self-deprecating in any way, even if it was hidden between the lines. Kiernan had given something very important away, but I wasn't quite sure what it was.

"I know you, Remy. More than you can possibly imagine."

"You recognize the feel of my magic. Don't try and deny it. I've been feeding it to you for some time now."

"I'm the one who gave you the ability to send yourself here to begin with. In essence, I saved your life that time, too."

Why? Why? Why? And how, for that matter? I tried to remember when I'd first discovered I had the ability to send myself bodily to Somniare. Part of that information was missing though. Did the laruas get it, or is it something more? It was a magical skill my mother had urged me to keep secret. She claimed others would be envious, and I'd believed her readily, but now I wasn't so sure. Did she know something I didn't? My mother did have the gift of premonition. But why would she allow a being such as Kiernan to feed me magic? Unless she knew that it would one day save my life. Maybe she'd been desperate to not lose another child after Callie's brutal murder. And then maybe she'd grown to resent me—all of it.

Or maybe she didn't know about Kiernan's magic at all.

But no matter what angle I looked at it, I was brought back around to ... Why the hell would Kiernan gift me with his magic to begin with? And why, when he'd been lurking around playing puppet master for so long, was he suddenly planning on laying all his cards on the table? None of it made sense, not really. All the known facts seemed to contradict each other. I most definitely didn't have all the pieces of the puzzle. So many damn questions.

Frustration vibrated through my bones, keeping me on edge. Rolling over, I stuffed my face into a pillow and screamed. I had to do something. I refused to just wait on Kiernan's whims. I wanted answers, sure, but I wasn't positive that any of them would make a difference in the grand scheme of things. No matter what he'd done for me, I wasn't granting Kiernan a favor by thanking him. In fact, I wasn't going to let him control me for one second longer. He'd been playing Machiavellian games, steering me since before I was murdered, and I wasn't going to stand for it.

I don't owe him for gifting me with something I didn't ask for. I didn't even know he existed until a few hours ago.

I flopped back over and stared at the ceiling, considering my options. Even though Kiernan had filled me to the brim with his magic—I could feel it buzzing underneath the surface of my skin—I still needed to conserve my energy so I didn't end up permanently dead. But I definitely felt more alive … vibrant. Surely, I had a bit to spare now, at least enough to free Unagi and Voo-Dolly, and hightail it out of Kiernan's lair.

Decision made.

Hefting myself up, I silently made my way across the small room, eyeing the far wall. Even though there wasn't a door there, I would make one. Raising my hands, I focused a minuscule amount of magic to create … "Voila! A door!" I ran my fingertips over my side and rejoiced to find I wasn't bleeding out. *Yes! Easy peasy! Suck it, Kiernan!*

I turned the knob, yanked the door open, and stepped through into—

My scream was swallowed by vast nothingness. It was as if my body was being forced to fit into a square peg, and I was in the shape of a circle. I bent and stretched, struggling to breathe. It was agonizing and endless ... until it did, in fact, end.

Sound filtered to me first. An acoustic guitar was being played, minor chords accompanying a soft voice.

"Melancholy sunshine,
Happy drops of rain,
Sometimes I just need the dark to hide my pain
And everything will be fine ..."

THEN CAME my sight and physical awareness. I was on my hands and knees in the middle of a bar, people standing all around me, gazes riveted on the girl performing on stage. I slowly pulled myself to my feet, my attention ensnared by the girl, too. Her voice, it was one I'd heard thousands of times in my dreams, one that I'd maybe only gotten to enjoy a quarter of that when she was actually alive.

"Callie!" Her name burst from my chest with longing and excitement. My sister was on stage performing. The song she was singing was new to me, but beautiful.

"Shhh!" Someone elbowed me in my side. I glanced to my right to see my mother standing there. Her dark hair was pulled back into a French braid, her clothes more casual than she usually wore; jeans and a red-checkered flannel.

"Mom?" Confusion washed over me. I couldn't remember how I'd gotten to the bar or what was going on. I'd known a moment ago, but now everything was fuzzy.

"I said to be quiet. Don't ruin this for Callie." My

mother's nails dug into my forearm and I gritted my teeth as the sharp tips broke my skin.

"But, Mom, something weird is going on. I don't know how I got here and I don't think—"

My mother's open palm cracked against the side of my face. "I told you to be quiet! Why do you have to ruin everything for Callie? You should have been the one who died, not her!"

I gasped, pressing my hand over my cheek, rubbing at the sting. I blinked rapidly, taking in my mother's furious expression. I'd never seen her quite so angry at me before. "I'm sorry."

"You should be." The knife glinted, catching my eye just before it slid into my gut. The agonizing, searing sensation hit me belatedly. I doubled over, grabbing at the blade protruding from my belly, my fingers slick with blood.

This can't be happening. This isn't right. Callie's dead. Not alive. None of this is real. And yet a part of me was caught up in the drama as if it was all very real. "Why?"

My mother turned away from me, as if I was nothing. I reached out for her just before I dropped to my knees. "Mom, help me."

"She said to be quiet," a masculine voice hissed from behind me. I didn't get a look at his face before something was rammed into my shoulder. *Did I just get stabbed again?*

I collapsed forward, and when I hit the ground, the knife in my stomach sank in farther. My vision wavered as I watched feet move past my helpless form, some of them pausing to kick me.

"Go ahead, Callie darling, your sister won't bother you anymore."

As if I didn't matter—as if I was nothing more than a piece of discarded trash—my sister started playing her song again, but with slightly different lyrics.

"*Melancholy sunshine,*

Happy drops of rain,

It all helps me hide the pain, but we all know Remy's to blame

For why I'll never be fine ..."

BLOOD BUBBLED UP, and dribbled from my lips, pooling on the floor in front of me as I mouthed the words along with her. My eyes fluttered shut. I should have died instead of Callie. She was everything wonderful, and ... and I'd never amount to even half of what she could have become. She'd been so talented at music, magic ... just about everything she attempted.

I remembered sitting on her bedroom floor and watching her, wanting so badly to be just like her when I grew up. I devoured any and all attention she would give me. Even the smallest hint of a smile thrown in my direction made me feel so special ... loved. I'd been positive my sister was the most amazing person in all of existence. And even though it'd been obvious since day one that my magic was stronger than hers, of who I'd be in Domus Novem, she'd never once been jealous, only supportive.

No. This isn't right. My sister loved me. And I loved her. Any parent would have been devastated after losing their eldest daughter. It wasn't Mom's fault how she became. It wasn't your fault either. This whole thing is wrong.

I forced my eyes open, finally remembering where I was. *Somniare.* It was strange how that had just oozed from my mind, causing me to get lost in my own personal nightmare, especially since no laruas were seemingly involved.

I staggered to my feet, the metallic tang of my blood coating my mouth. For one moment, merely an instant in time, I allowed my gaze to linger on my sister, even though I knew it wasn't really her. Her tall, graceful form was perched on a wooden stool, her dark hair spilling halfway down her back. She wore faded jeans and a black tank top, her feet bare, just like mine. It was the outfit she'd been murdered in, and the irony that I was wearing my death attire as well wasn't lost on me. In fact, my sister and I looked so much alike now; she'd been the same age as me when her life had been cut short. It was something I hadn't considered until just then. Both of us murdered at seventeen—there had to be some kind of connection, something I'd have to consider at a later time since I knew no answers would be forthcoming from a nightmare conjured in Somniare.

I mourned the loss of Callie, something I did every day, even if not completely consciously. I'd only been five years old when she'd been ripped away from our family, but she'd been my everything in a way only an older sister can be. I'd always suspected, because of the age gap, that I hadn't been planned, and yes, some part of me wondered if my parents had wished that I'd been the one stolen from them instead of Callie. The only reason I wasn't completely invisible to them was because of my standing within Domus Novem. You can't exactly ignore the next Grand Witch. I lived a life full of guilt and regret, existing in the ever-present shadow of my dead sister. It had hardened and jaded me, closed me off on some level. But seeing her, even a mere facsimile, tore open old wounds, gouging my heart.

"She deserved life. You don't." I was shoved forward roughly, but I refused to topple over. I latched onto the nearest person's shirt, staggering into them.

If I could have traded places with Callie, given my life for hers, then I would have in a heartbeat, but I couldn't change the past. Callie died, and I lived, that's just the way it was. The sorrow I felt for my sister's loss would never fade, I knew that, but I could move past the regret, I had to. That's the thing about emotional pain—you can stuff it down deep, lock it away, and force yourself not to feel it. Emotional pain won't actually hurt you, if you don't let it. *At least outside of Somniare, that is.*

I wrenched the blade from my stomach, crying out as it slid free. I trickled just enough magic into the wound to staunch the bleeding, hoping it would be enough to sustain me until more could be done.

A sea of sneering faces turned towards me, hateful eyes tracking my every movement. I dropped into a fighting stance, the knife in my shoulder shifting painfully. The mob descended on me, intent on blood—my blood. I slashed and stabbed with my right hand, burying the knife in flesh and then tearing, coating the room in crimson. My left arm I kept up and out, letting it take the brunt of my attackers' blows.

Somehow I managed to take everyone out, littering the floor with bodies. Most of what I did was a blur, adrenaline fueling deathblow after deathblow, coupled with the training I'd had drilled into me since I was a child. I didn't let my thoughts linger on what I'd done, since technically none of it was real. *But it feels real. So real.* Instead, I staggered to the stage, slumping over as I stared up at the now empty stool. *At least I didn't have to fight Callie.*

I groaned, my fingers loosening, and the knife clattered to the ground just before I joined it.

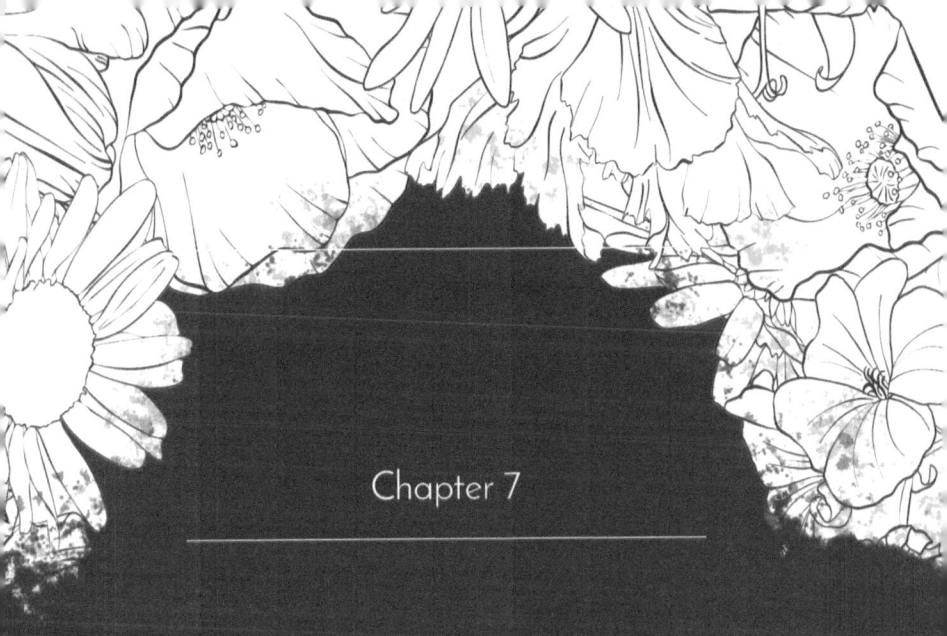

Chapter 7

"**S**uch a stubborn *cailleach*."

I gasped, sitting straight up. My gaze darted around warily, taking in my surroundings as my brain filtered through everything that happened just before I—what? Passed out? Died? I didn't even know what was possible in Somniare anymore. All I knew was that I seemed to be whole again. And right back where I started.

I groaned. "You've got to be kidding me. I went through all of that and here I am … again."

"You're lucky I found you when I did." Kiernan lowered himself slowly, perching on the end of the large bed. "You—"

"Let's cut the crap, fae. I'm tired of your games. I want answers and you're going to give them to me."

"Stubborn—"

"You say stubborn, I say desperate. And desperate

times call for desperate measures. I just want to get the hell out of Somniare in one piece." It was then I noticed that I was no longer wearing the blue dress I'd been stuck in since arriving in Somniare. I was naked—completely and utterly without one stitch of clothing. Thankfully, I was under a sheet. Although not much, it was something.

"Not desperate enough to thank me ... yet."

His words barely registered. "You undressed me?" I pulled the sheet up higher, directing my narrowed gaze at the shadows within Kiernan's dark hood. "Give me back my clothes right now!"

"You were covered in blood. It looked like you'd bathed in gore. I—"

"With all your magic, you couldn't have taken care of that? Instead, you had to undress me? And not give me some new stuff to wear? Seriously? Hope you looked your fill because you're never gonna get another show from me, pervert."

Kiernan stood abruptly, his body rigid. "Is it possible for you to not be so bloody confrontational for one bloody second? Or is that too much for you to handle? You're not going to make it out of Somniare without my help. You need to—"

"You know what? Screw my clothes." I threw the sheet back and stood, goose bumps erupting in quick succession across my skin. "I'd rather run around naked than sit here and listen to your arrogant fae ass. I don't need your help."

"How many times will I have to save your life before you admit that you can't do everything yourself? Asking for assistance is not a weakness. Pretending to not need anyone—that you don't have any weaknesses at all—that's what truly makes you vulnerable."

Ignoring him, I stepped to the right to go around him. He moved to block me. I stepped to the left, and he countered. "Get out of my way."

"No." His voice had dropped a few octaves, causing me to shiver.

I ground my teeth together, pretending not to notice that I could feel Kiernan's gaze slowly dancing up my naked body. "Don't make me use my magic on you." I lifted my hands, my fingers resembling claws.

"You mean *my* magic?" He chuckled. "All you'd accomplish is needing me to give you more. But maybe you'd like that, hmmm? Maybe you crave feeling a part of me moving within you?"

Now there was the typical fae arrogance I'd come to expect from his race. "Please," I scoffed. "You never take that hood off because it's stuck over your ginormous, ego-swollen head, and you can't."

"You want answers, then you'll stay."

I sniffed. "I don't really want them anymore." *Lie. Lie. Lie.* I really, really wanted them. But I could do without them if I had to. I'd gone for seventeen years without the information I now craved, therefore none of it seemed to be imperative to my survival. *At least not yet.* And that's what got me, the little niggling of doubt. What if the information Kiernan could give me was important to my future? What if not having it was what got me murdered to begin with? And what if he had the answers that would help me ultimately survive? *Damnit!*

I lifted my head and crossed my arms over my chest. "I want clothes, now, and let Unagi and Voo-Dolly out of that cage. Unagi's my familiar—I think you know what that means. Then maybe I'll stay long enough for you to give me some answers."

Kiernan stiffened. "I think you're forgetting who's holding all the cards here."

"Nope, it's me. So … deal?"

"No." Kiernan snapped his fingers and suddenly I was back on the bed but with one big difference—I was now tethered to it by ropes around my wrists and ankles.

"This isn't the way to get what you want," I gritted out, thrashing against the bonds.

"Neither is acting like a child." Kiernan disappeared.

My breath whooshed out of me audibly as I willed my body to stop shaking. Despite my bravado, Kiernan scared me. And I was also naked. Or maybe I was scared because I was naked? Nothing like nudity to heighten the fear-factor of being around a large male with tons of magical abilities. The truth was, Kiernan could roll my mind and make me beg for him to touch me in any way he wanted. It wouldn't be the first time a fae had taken advantage of a less-than-willing female. With egos as large as theirs, it was like they couldn't comprehend anyone, male or female, not wanting them. They didn't understand rape for that reason, which was utterly terrifying.

I turned my head to study the ropes. I already knew

they were magically reinforced. Kiernan's wild flavor of magic hummed against my skin. *Think. Think. Think. There has to be something I can do.*

And then it hit me. I wasn't sure it would work, but I had nothing to lose by trying.

I closed my eyes and focused on the magic twisted through the fibers of the ropes. It was there between the molecules that made up the bindings, but it wasn't part of it. The molecules and magic merely danced side-by-side, not attached on a fundamental level. When magic wasn't a part of something, and merely co-existed, when given the chance, it flowed to like magic. It was one of the basic laws I'd learned as a child. Like magic calls to like magic. And I just so happened to have a crap-load of Kiernan's magic inside of me. *Come to Mama.*

I tugged with my mind, sucking all the luscious energy right into me, giving me a slight jolt. *Better than coffee.* With a smile, I then directed what I'd stolen back at the ropes, disintegrating them. I'd managed to not waste a single drop of what I needed to maintain my quasi-life in Somniare.

Ha! You'll have to do better than that you stupid arrogant fae! I rolled off the bed, grinning to myself. Although there was still the matter of clothes. *Shit.* Those I couldn't do anything about. I really didn't want to use any more magic in case—or rather, for *when* I'd need it later. Plus, I was going to need a bit to get out of the room to begin with. If I was going to make a run from Kiernan, I couldn't count on him to fix me up anymore. I had very little magic to spare, a pittance really.

I'd have to improvise creating clothes. I scanned the room for options, my eyes lingering on the bed. Yanking the sheet off, I tied it around me like a toga. *Not ideal, but it'll work.*

I strode over to the wall and eyed it speculatively. The first time I'd attempted conjuring a door I'd ended up in a nightmare where I'd gotten knifed—repeatedly. Not something I wanted to repeat. One of the problems with doing magic in Somniare was that I didn't have some of the checks and balances I did in the real world. For instance, when I did a spell wrong, normally, I got a bitter flavor on the tip of my tongue, as if I could taste a problem in the magic itself. The spell that had taken me to my nightmare had definitely been wrong, and yet I hadn't sensed it.

Maybe I just needed to use a bit more magic and a lot more intent. I raised my hands, concentrating on Unagi. A door, identical in appearance to the one I'd created during my last escape, loomed in front of me. I swallowed, my throat suddenly dry, and reached for the handle. *Please be right this time.*

"I wouldn't." Kiernan's hot breath teased my bare shoulder.

Without sparing him a glance, I grabbed the handle and stepped through the frame.

"Yeah, well you're not me," I said.

Chapter 8

Cold. *So cold. Never been so cold.* Ice clung to my body, sheets of it, making it nearly impossible to move. I staggered forward by sheer force of will, my feet completely numb.

"You will all bow down before me, for I am your God now!"

The frigid air burned my lungs as I sucked in a ragged breath through cracked lips. I lifted my gaze, realizing that I wasn't alone. A crowd of people, disheveled humans of all shapes and sizes, huddled together, all staring at a figure atop the mountain directly in front of us.

"You all serve me now!"

The wind picked up and the crowd collectively shuddered. Between the snow and ice pelting me in the face, I couldn't make out more than a vague silhouette of the male. He was large and wearing dark robes that whipped nefariously in the wind.

Hello, cliché villain.

"Who are you?" The words escaped before I had the chance to consider them. It usually wasn't a bright idea to draw attention to yourself when it came to insane creatures, even if they were only part of another Somniare nightmare.

A low rumble of a laugh danced through the air, eerie in how beautiful and warm it sounded in comparison to the glacial setting. "Well, well, well, aren't you a surprise. I didn't expect to find you here." The familiarity in his tone set me on edge.

"Do I know you?"

"Ah, the laruas did manage to take some, but not all. Not nearly enough."

A hand clamped down on my shoulder, startling a scream from me, much to my shame. "What—"

I collapsed in a sodden heap on the floor of the room where Unagi and Voo-Dolly were being held. Although the bone-deep chill was miraculously gone, I rubbed my arms and legs ferociously, heaving a sigh of relief. I wasn't sure what my little foray into ice-land had been about, but I was safe now and I'd somehow managed to end up where I wanted to be after all.

"Remy!"

"Mama!"

I lurched to my feet, sliding in a puddle when I rushed forward. I stopped just short of touching the enchanted bars. With narrowed eyes, I glanced behind me. "Where the hell is Kiernan?"

"How should I know?" Unagi's tails tapped against the ground, spelling out annoyance with each swish.

"He was with me before I walked through the door. I thought for sure he'd come after me."

"Don't look a gift horse in the mouth. Get me out of here before you get the answer to your question."

I shook my head, dislodging the mush that had my brain focusing on all the wrong things. "Right. Okay. How exactly do I do that?"

Unagi jerked its fox head to the right. "How about using the key?"

My eyes widened in surprise. "That definitely wasn't there before."

"Again, gift horse."

I ground my teeth together. "Stop giving me attitude. I risked my life to save you. Is it the name thing still?"

Unagi sighed heavily. "I'm sorry, okay? There are just things—things I can't tell you about. They have me on edge."

"What kind of things?" I grabbed the large, ornate key and stuck it in the lock, turning it quickly. The red glow emanating from the bars flickered briefly before softening in intensity.

"I just said I couldn't tell you." Unagi moved through the small opening the door provided, its fox form flickering wildly. "We need to—" Unagi collapsed face first to the ground, the fox replaced by the same male warrior I'd seen once before, his lithe form covered in a black and white kimono. Unagi groaned loudly as he attempted to push himself up, his arms shaking with the effort.

I dropped down beside him, my knees hitting the ground with a thud. "What's wrong? What's happening?"

Voo-Dolly pressed against my hip, her small cloth hand wrapping around my wrist. "Mama, I can help." She pulled a pin out of her side and stretched towards Unagi.

"Stop, keep that thing away from me," Unagi muttered, the side of his face pressed into the ground.

"Talk to me then." I smoothed his silken locks off of his forehead so I could get a better look into his eyes. "Tell me what's going on with you."

"The cage drained m-magic ..." His lavender gaze shuttered, his eyelids snapping closed abruptly.

"Mama?" Voo-Dolly glanced up at me with question, her small hand still extended with the pin. *So why didn't the cage drain Voo-Dolly's magic, too? Very curious indeed.*

"What will it do?"

"Give Unagi some magic. Just a little. If I give too much I won't be real anymore."

"Oh." That raised some more very interesting questions. Of course, it wasn't the time to delve into that topic, not with my familiar lying vulnerable on the floor.

I studied Unagi. He appeared to be sleeping, his back rising and falling in a steady pattern. He'd probably replenish his magic naturally ... eventually, but we didn't have the time to wait around for that to happen. "Do it."

Voo-Dolly jabbed the pin into the base of Unagi's skull, thrusting it in and yanking it back quickly. A dot of blood bloomed on his neck, the pin still pristine. "What the—" Unagi pushed up and skittered across the floor, his eyes wide and hand covering the back of his neck. "I told you to keep that thing away from me."

Smiling, I patted Voo-Dolly on the head. "Good job. I'm proud of you." The small sewn-on smile stretched wide with glee.

"Proud of her? Do you have any idea—"

A new door swung open, ice and snow swirling towards us from within. Kiernan's leather-clad figure appeared in silhouette, his gloved hands latched onto the frame as he tried to pull himself through. "Help. Me," he hissed, as if in pain.

I stared slack jawed. *Help him?* He was abruptly yanked back, a cold blast of air whipping through the room. I rushed forward on instinct, my bare feet slapping the ground painfully. Kiernan was no longer visible, and I froze in place when I saw what was heading straight for us —laruas, at least ten of them. *Shit. I need to get the door closed.* When just pushing at it didn't work, I raised my hands, magic pulsing in my palms.

"Remy, no!" Unagi yelled, barely loud enough for me to hear over the roaring wind. "I don't have anything left to give you."

My mind rifled rapidly through options, coming up with none. At least it'd be a better choice to die all the way than become a larua. I narrowed my eyes with determination. Something metallic clattered at my feet, stealing my attention.

"Use it, not your magic," Unagi commanded.

Without hesitation, I swooped down to pick up the katana. As soon as my fingers made contact, magic jolted my system, fusing with mine. Bright white light flashed, temporarily blinding me. As I blinked away the dancing spots from my vision, I realized I was encased in some kind of translucent armor from head to toe. It shimmered faintly as I flexed, exploring the sensation of having it around me. It was feather light and felt almost like a second skin, although there was a bit of distance between it and my actual flesh and clothes. The armor's magic connected me to it in some unseen way, making it move fluidly with every motion I made. A sudden feeling of déjà-vu washed over me, but I shook it off, focusing on the now.

Pulling myself up to my full height, I stood with my feet wide, head held high, and bared my teeth. "Come and get it."

The laruas swarmed me, but I was ready. A step to the right, a pirouette, a lunge to the left … it was almost like dancing. With each slice of the luminescent sword, I cut away at the darkness—the vast nothingness that made up my foes. I giggled with glee as the last larua evaporated with one final thrust into its churning middle, and the door slammed shut on its own accord.

"I did it!" I lifted the katana in victory, doing a little jig. But my jubilation was short lived as I began to process what had just happened. I pivoted in Unagi's direction, glaring at him. "Why didn't you use the sword before?

And how did I know what to do, how to use it? It all felt so … so—"

"We're bonded—you and me. So my sword recognized you." Unagi had propped himself up in a sitting position against the wall, with his head tilted back. He was awake, but he definitely looked a bit worse for the wear.

"And why didn't you use it before on the laruas?"

"Tarik is temperamental. He was angry with me about something and he wouldn't come when I called him before."

I blinked several times and glanced down at the katana, taking the time to study it. The glow that had been surrounding it in battle had faded, but the sword didn't look any less special. The handle—or whatever that part of a katana is called—was covered with ornate silver carvings, and what appeared to be spun gold interwoven around them. The blade itself glistened as if made of liquid silver. There was no doubt that if a sword deserved a name, this one did.

"So the katana is sentient?" It wouldn't be the first time I'd heard of inanimate objects being *more* in the magic world.

"Yes."

"And it only comes to you when it feels like it?"

"Pretty much."

"And it came to you now because?"

Sighing, Unagi closed his eyes. "Because I had no other way of helping you."

"So he likes me?" Tarik lit up as if answering my question himself. I grinned.

Unagi glared at the glowing katana, his forehead beading with sweat. "Don't get too excited. He's fickle." Tarik vibrated, turning red. "Well, you are and you know it." With a loud popping noise Tarik disappeared, taking my armor with him.

"Why'd you go and piss him off?" I crossed my arms over my chest, hating that I was wearing nothing but a damp sheet again.

"Told you, temperamental." Unagi slumped to the side, unconscious once again.

Chapter 9

"We can't just wait around for Kiernan to come back so he can lock us up again."

I paced back and forth across the tiny room, one end to the other, and then back again. Rinse and repeat. Unagi was resting peacefully, his color returning slowly. My worry for his condition had faded, positive his magic just needed to recharge. Voo-Dolly watched me with a forlorn expression since her pittance of magic didn't do anything in the way of conjuring a way out of the room. Nor did it revive Unagi a second time. "I have to do something, damnit!"

I was beyond frustrated, and a little bit scared. *What if Kiernan's dead? And then what if Unagi never charges up enough to get us out of here? Without Kiernan to free us, we could spend all of eternity in this room. Or I could die using up all of my magic trying to escape.* "Aaaah! There has to be something I can do!"

Dropping down to sit against the wall beside Unagi, I studied his beautiful face, wondering if the visage I was staring at was his true form. He claimed gender ambiguity, but he had to have been born one or the other, right? Or maybe all kitsunes were like Unagi, both male and female? I just couldn't help but be curious. I knew so little about kitsunes in general.

"What about Tarik? Maybe he can help?" I mused, gaze still locked on Unagi. His eyes moved rapidly behind his closed lids. What if he was trapped in a nightmare? *Crap. I need to do something!*

Goose bumps erupted across my flesh as a cool breeze swirled through the room. It was emanating from a small crack in the wall, illuminated by a sliver of light. I pulled myself up and crept forward on the balls of my feet, the scent of roses twisting around me, luring me. I cautiously curled my fingers into the fissure, tugging gently. A door appeared, creaking open enough for me to peer through. I gripped the edge of the warm wood, my knuckles whitening. I inhaled sharply, not having expected to see such beauty, not after the snow and laruas.

Before me was a lush garden, vines of blood-red roses entangled around everything as far as I could see. And fluttering from flower to flower, their wings shimmering in the subdued sunshine, were thousands of magnificent butterflies, their colors vibrant shades of blue and purple.

I bit my lower lip, considering our situation. Very few things in Somniare were what they seemed, and I knew the scene before me would probably be no different. The real question was: would we be better off chancing the unknown, or waiting where it was safe?

I glanced over my shoulder at Unagi and Voo-Dolly. Neither of them would be much good to me, and yet I knew I wouldn't leave either of them behind. *Morally ambiguous my ass.* The pre-Somniare me would have ditched them both in a heartbeat, but some of my carefully erected walls had developed cracks because of the memories I'd faced of my sister. I didn't like the new me one bit. She was more vulnerable—weak even.

Closing my eyes, I rubbed my temples. I knew what I should do, but unfortunately, I seldom listened to even my own advice.

I shoved the door open all the way, praying to the gods it would stay that way long enough for me to drag Unagi through it. I then eyed my familiar speculatively, considering the best way to transport him, knowing he'd be dead weight. Shrugging, I grabbed his ankles and yanked him forward, cringing when his head thumped against the ground. "Sorry," I muttered.

"Mama?"

"Don't worry, Voo-Dolly, I got this."

It was slow going dragging Unagi across the floor, me having little traction in my bare feet. I kept imagining him waking up to yell at me for what I was doing, but he slept on, soft snores escaping his parted lips. In repose, he appeared so innocent, and peaceful. My heart squeezed in remorse for something I couldn't quite put my finger on. *Why does it feel like I'm angry at Unagi for something I can't remember?* Which would be plausible considering the laruas, if not for the fact that I hadn't met Unagi until after I'd been attacked by them. *You can't lose what isn't there to start with. And yet ... Something's missing. I can feel the hole where it should be.*

With a final grunt of exertion, I made it through the door with Unagi, Voo-Dolly dashing after us. I flopped down on the damp grass, staring at the sky. Butterflies flitted around us. I knew it wasn't the best plan, just like all of my ideas lately, but I couldn't seem to keep my eyes open.

"I won't fall asleep. I'm just going to rest for a minute," I murmured, not sure if I was talking to Voo-Dolly or myself.

Of course I knew it was a lie.

I was asleep as soon as my lids slid shut.

"I KNOW THIS IS YOU. *I know they're both you. I do. But what you don't seem to get is that I'll take either ... or both. Just please don't say neither. Never say neither.*"

I jerked up into a sitting position, words from a dream swimming through my mind. Which baffled me because I didn't think it possible to have a normal dream in Somniare. Was it something else? It didn't feel like it.

I stretched and yawned as I let my gaze roam over Unagi, who was still out cold. Voo-Dolly was noticeably absent, but I wasn't too concerned. She seemed to be able to take care of herself. Or at least she'd done fine so far.

"Hey," a masculine voice rumbled from behind me.

I whirled around, my gaze landing on the same asshat that had gotten all gropey with me in the neon forest. He was leaning against a tree a couple of feet away, his muscular arms crossed over his chest. "You better stay away from me if you know what's good for you." I raised my hands in a threat of magical assault. Obviously it was a bluff, but there was no way he could know that.

"Look, about earlier—"

"Oh, you mean when you stuck your tongue down my throat and groped me within five seconds of meeting me —without my permission? That earlier?"

"I didn't know! I thought you were just a dream."

I scowled, considering. It was highly plausible, if not most likely. "And how do you know I'm not a dream now?"

He ran his hand over his short-cropped hair, his cheeks coloring slightly. "I've been here, wherever here is, for a long while. Too long. I thought all of this was a dream, and maybe you are, too. But dream or not, you got me feelin' guilty about before, darlin'."

I motioned to the garden and butterflies. "This your dream? Or are you trespassing, looking for me?" Dreamers could, in theory, cross into each other's dreamscapes. I wasn't sure if it was a common thing, or what made it possible, but it could happen.

"This is mine. So was the one before. Don't ask me

why I'm always dreamin' 'bout such things. I've never been much about trees and flowers, and yet they keep on poppin' up 'round me here."

"When you say you've been here a long while, how long do you think it's been?" My perception of time was skewed in Somniare, so there was no way of telling if anyone's was any better, but I was curious about how self-aware of his dreaming this particular human seemed to be.

"I don't know, really. Feels like forever if I'm bein' honest." He pushed off the tree and took a few steps towards me. When I tensed, he stopped and raised his hands in surrender. "I'll keep my distance this time, darlin'."

I uncurled myself from the grassy knoll I'd been napping on and lumbered to my feet, crossing my arms over my chest. "I'd appreciate it if you'd stop calling me *darlin'*." I rolled the term of endearment over my tongue with an exaggerated Southern accent, mocking him. "I'm definitely not your darlin' or anyone else's for that matter."

He shrugged. "It's just what us southern boys are raised to do. I'll try n' stop, but it comes natural to someone like me. It's not meant to disrespect, quite the opposite."

It was then I noticed that I was back in the blue dress I'd been murdered in. "What the hell?" I grabbed at the gauzy material with annoyance. "You've got to be kidding me." It was as if new—no bloodstains or tears. Although, I supposed it was better than wearing a sheet.

"You don't like the dress?"

I glanced up at military-boy and frowned. "No. If I never see another dress again, it'll be too soon."

He raised his eyebrows and chuckled. "It suits you so well though. You have the whole Snow White thing down."

I glanced at my exposed flesh and cringed. I was a bit paler than usual, being that I was only quasi-alive, but Snow White, really? "Yeah, well this isn't a fairytale and I'm not a princess." I blinked rapidly, staring down the line of my body. The dress was no longer there. In its place was a worn pair of jeans, and a faded white T-shirt. I wiggled my toes in the beat-up pair of cowboy boots. It was definitely a step in the right direction. "You do this?"

"Yep. Name's Owen, by the way."

"I don't remember asking for an introduction." I was definitely softening towards him, though, especially since he genuinely seemed like a decent guy. The whole groping thing ... well, what red-blooded male wouldn't grope a girl who he was attracted to that just popped up in his dream? Plus, I didn't see any other humans around that I could hitch a ride out of Somniare with. However, I was going to have to play things just right. If I switched moods too quickly, Owen would know I was up to something. Just because he talked slow didn't mean he was stupid.

"Aw, come on, darlin'. I told you I meant no harm before. Can't we just be friends?"

"There you go with the darlin' again."

"Sorry."

"But I get it … whatever. I guess I can forgive you for all of it, since it was a mistake, and you did conjure up these clothes for me." I let a smile tug my lips up, as if it was reluctant. "I'm Remy."

"And who's sleeping beauty?" Owen nodded in Unagi's direction.

I chuckled. "You have a thing for fairy tales, huh?" My gaze roamed over my familiar with tenderness. "That's Unagi."

"He your man?"

I sputtered on a laugh, the air lodging in my chest. "He's not a man at all." I gasped for breath. "He's a kitsune, and a gender ambiguous one at that." I wasn't really sure why I was laughing when it was as if something inside of me was weeping. My emotions were jumbled, and I didn't know what to think of my reaction.

"Gender ambiguous? Kitsune? I feel like we're speakin' a different language."

I sobered, meeting Owen's gaze. "You serious about wanting to be friends?"

He nodded, not breaking eye contact. "Yeah, I'm serious."

"Okay, good." I motioned for him to come closer. "Then I suppose I have a few things to explain to you."

Chapter 10

I lied, of course.

I couldn't exactly tell Owen that I wanted to hitch a ride with him out of Somniare, and the result would ultimately be his death. Instead, I told him that giving me a ride would cause him no harm. I just didn't have a way out of Somniare myself because of my murder. He was taking the rest in stride as well, the part about Unagi and me being magical creatures.

"So how exactly do I take you with me?" Owen asked, his gaze roaming my features. We were sitting under a tree, him leaning against it with one leg propped up, and his arms loose at his sides. I was sitting cross-legged beside him.

"There should be some kind of door which is personal to you in your dreamscape. And it doesn't actually have to be a door. But when you enter it or jump through it—

whatever you need to do for whatever it is—you'll wake up. The next time you go, you simply take me with you."

Owen flicked his gaze away. "Maybe that's why I haven't woken up, because I don't know what or where my door is."

"How can you not know?" I leaned in closer, worry flipping my stomach. If he didn't know how to find his way out of Somniare, he was no good to me. *Maybe that's why Unagi didn't lead me to him. Maybe something's wrong with Owen.* I spared a glance at my slumbering familiar. He still showed no signs of waking. *And where the hell is Voo-Dolly?* She'd been gone for entirely too long, and I was starting to get worried.

"I told you, I've been here for a while. Maybe that's why. Maybe I need to figure out how to wake up."

"What was the last thing you remember from before you came here?"

Own scratched his head, lost in thought. He was silent a few moments before he cleared his throat and spoke, "I was out on a mission, I think. And then ..." He scrubbed a hand down his face. "And then I was here."

I chewed on the inside of my cheek, studying him. He'd told me he was a soldier, which I'd already guessed from his attire. Was it possible he was in some kind of coma? "A mission? Do you remember if you were hurt?"

He shook his head in frustration. "It's all a bit fuzzy, darlin'. Sorry."

I contained the sigh that wanted to escape from me. I didn't know if Owen was a lost cause or not. *I suppose I could try to help him find his way out. It's not like I've been tripping over humans lately.* "I'll help you find your way out. It'll be a win-win for us." I crossed my fingers behind my back and smiled.

Unagi groaned, long and loud. I was on my feet instantly, rushing to his side. I dropped to my knees, my hands fluttering around his face and chest. "Can you hear me? How do you feel?"

His lids peeled open slowly, and the lavender of his eyes flashed gold. "Rems," he murmured, raising his hand to cup my cheek.

I pressed into his touch, the contact warming me in places it shouldn't have. "Unagi." I bit my lower lip. Something was different about his reaction to me. It was unguarded and intimate, causing my heart to thrash against my ribcage.

"Unagi?" Confusion rolled across his features, bringing with it ... anger? Frustration? Ripping his hand away, he turned his head. "Give me a minute."

"Why? Is there something I can—"

"I said to give me a minute!" he yelled, curling onto his side, chest heaving.

I stood slowly, bewildered. "O-okay." I stared at his back, fighting the urge to go to him and push the issue.

"I can't change," Unagi whispered.

"What?"

He flopped onto his back, eyes panicked. "My magic hasn't recharged enough for me to change forms."

"Okay. But it will soon, right? It's not a big deal—"

"It's a huge deal. I can't change!" Lightning fast, he moved into a crouch, his teeth flashing as he grimaced. "I can't stay like this."

"Why not? It'll be just for a little bit."

"I can't." He pressed his hands into his temples and squeezed his eyes shut. "I just can't."

"Unagi, please. You're overreacting."

He relaxed, his eyes opening to snare my gaze again, holding it the entire time as he rose. When he stood at his full height, a good couple of inches taller than me, he approached at a snail's pace, one heavy footstep at a time. He halted directly in front of me, scant inches away, our breath intermingling.

I inhaled sharply, unsure of how to react. My mind and body weren't on the same page. My mind was screaming at me to back up, to run away, but my body wanted closer —ever so closer. "Talk to me, Unagi. Why are you freaking out?"

He chuckled, the sound completely without humor. "I can't stay like this around you."

"Why not?"

"Because I feel too much like ... like a male when I am." His fingers ran slowly up my arms, dancing along my bare flesh sensually. I shivered, swaying into him. His spicy and rich scent, which was different with each form he was in, wrapped me in desire. The fabric of his kimono was damp, and when he pressed into me farther, I found the coolness it offered welcome against my overheated skin.

"Unagi," I murmured, his name rolling off my tongue with reverence.

His fingers dug into my arms painfully as he yanked me away from him, putting a few inches of distance between us. "But I'm not a male, not really."

"You look and feel like one to me." I pressed into him again before his grip tightened even more.

"For all intents and purposes, I am a male while I'm in this form. But I'm both this and the female you saw before. I'm both, Remy." His gaze pleaded with me to back off, and I knew I should, but something was driving me on —urging me to push him to his limits.

"Why does it matter if you're both? Your mind and heart are always the same no matter what form you're in, right? You know I'm attracted to males and females—if you want me as a male, you'll want me as a female, too." *What am I saying? Why am I pushing this?* Unagi would always be my familiar, and a sexual relationship with one's familiar was taboo. The bond was supposed to transcend the flesh. *Back off, Remy. Back the hell off before you do something you'll regret.*

Unagi flung me away from him, but I managed to snag his arm before he could get past me. My thumb ran over a pattern of rough skin on the interior of his wrist, the symmetry of it— "What's this?"

Unagi's lavender eyes flashed with panic, bleeding to black. "Let go."

"How is this possible?" I didn't need to see the mark to know exactly what it was. It was the symbol for Domus

Novem. Similar to a Celtic knot in appearance, the curves twisted into nine points. This particular mark had one difference that made it more than just a Novem brand—within the center was my personal spell signature, what looked like a fancy letter R curling through the lopsided pattern.

"It's not what you think."

"No? Then tell me what it is." After a witch and familiar bonded fully, the witch, with the familiar's permission of course, placed a magical brand somewhere on the being; again, the familiar's choice. For Unagi to already wear my brand was impossible. *Completely and utterly impossible. Isn't it?*

"It's Somniare. Things are different between us because of Somniare. You've accepted me as your familiar so the mark appeared. It doesn't actually exist."

With narrowed eyes, I studied Unagi's face for clues. His expression was utterly bland. It seemed ... plausible, but I didn't trust him. And that fact did something weird to my insides. Everything between us was off—wrong. "Can I trust you?"

Before I processed what was happening, I was cocooned in Unagi's arms, my face pressed into his strong chest. "You can trust that I will do what's best for you. Always."

I knew it wasn't the same thing. He'd chosen his words carefully for a reason, but I also knew he wasn't going to reveal why. My familiar was definitely keeping secrets—big secrets. "Tell me what you're hiding." I pushed at his mind, but it was sealed off, just like every time I attempted to probe.

His arms slid down my body, trembling as if he never wanted to let me go. "We just need distance while I'm in my original male or female form. I just need distance."

I bit my tongue before I could ask why again, my thoughts flittering over both of his original forms. I wouldn't kick either of them out of my bed. *Wait, what? Unagi may be the same on the inside in either form, but you don't know his heart and mind—neither of them. You don't know him, or her.* And yet something inside of me screamed out that I did.

I was the one who finally broke our embrace, despite Unagi's claim of wanting space. I gnawed on my thumbnail, careful not to meet his gaze again. "Explain to me the whole male female thing. You had to have been born one or the other. I want to understand." He kept implying I didn't, and I wanted to know … everything about him.

"Yeah, I want to understand, too."

"Owen!" I gasped, whirling in his direction. I'd somehow managed to completely forget about him.

"Remy?" Unagi's voice rose in question. Obviously, he hadn't noticed Owen either, us being so caught up in our little melodrama.

I waved my hand behind me. "It's fine. He explained himself. He thought I was a dream before. But—" I glanced over my shoulder just as Unagi brandished Tarik. "I see he came this time. Why?"

Unagi grunted, not answering, his furious gaze leveled on Owen, Tarik glowing red.

"Whoa, whoa, whoa." Owen raised his hands in surrender. "I didn't mean her any harm. Her and me talked things out while you were sleepin'."

"Don't hurt him. I need him to get out of here. You know this." Unagi remained quiet, his stance appearing relaxed, but I knew better. "Unagi, I mean it. Don't hurt him."

He heaved a huge sigh, and Tarik disappeared, going wherever it was sentient swords went when not with their owners. "All kitsune are both male and female. Which sex they appear as when born is like flipping a coin. The other side is still there even if you can't see it right away. We are harmony, a balance of the male and female energies, yin and yang all rolled into one. Today's generations, supernatural and human alike, are so obsessed with proving that females can do what males can do that they're losing what makes them uniquely special. Females weren't created to do everything a male can do, females were created to do everything a male can't, and vice versa. The sexes balance each other out … which is why I'm perfect. Kitsune are the only perfect beings in all of existence—half female and half male, able to call on whichever side is best suited for whatever task at hand."

Wow. That doesn't sound like he's spit out that little speech a million times before. Not at all. And perfect being? Get over yourself. Although …

He cleared his throat and ensnared my gaze before he

said the next part. "Kitsune—the rare ones who mate—usually do so with other kitsune for that reason. It's difficult to find someone who both sides want equally. It's easier with another kitsune."

What was he trying to say? That the female part of him didn't want me? Because I was pretty sure the male part of him did. "But it could happen? It's not outside the realm of possibility for a kitsune to want just one person—for both sides to want the same thing?"

Unagi's jaw muscles popped as he ground his teeth together, his nostrils flaring with agitation. He opened his mouth to answer my question, and I sucked in a breath, waiting.

But he never got the chance to answer, not before we were all dropped into pitch-blackness.

Chapter 11

The lights rose slowly, like we were in a play, and Unagi and I found ourselves smack dab in the middle of a military operation, Owen nowhere in sight. Crumbling brick buildings surrounded us, sand and dirt clinging to everything, including the inside of my nose and mouth. It looked like a scene straight from a video game, complete with guys in military uniforms rushing past us to get to prime positions.

A bullet whizzed past my head, but instead of exhibiting any kind of self-preservation, I was propelled to wage war, anger blistering my veins. Tarik, favoring me once more, appeared in my hand, glowing as if filled by the light from a thousand stars. I charged forward, ignoring Unagi's pleas for me to stop, striking down bullets from mid-air with nothing but a katana. It was exhilarating, and the laughter that bubbled up and burst from my chest buoyed my mood.

"You'll have to do better than that!" I yelled at the unseen enemy. A few more bullets pinged off Tarik. "You know how someone can check to see if they're a bad guy or not? If you have poor aim, then you're on the wrong side of good!" I giggled at my own joke.

I'd been worried from the beginning about losing my mind in Somniare. But I didn't have to concern myself anymore...

It's too late. I'm utterly mad.

"Remy! Get back here!" Unagi scurried after me, deftly dodging bullets without aid from Tarik, or the magical armor currently encasing me.

"No! I'm having fun!" I swung Tarik in an arc, hitting more bullets from the air. They just kept coming and coming, but it didn't matter, I was invincible.

"It's Tarik! He's influencing you! You're too weak to separate your feelings from his! You're letting him take control!"

I pondered his words while I continued to play. What Unagi said held a ring of truth to it. Hadn't I felt overzealous about the battle with the laruas the last time Tarik had appeared to me? *Maybe I'm not mad after all.* But then again— "I like feeling this way. No worries, no fear. I don't care if it's not me."

When the deluge of bullets paused, Unagi took the opportunity to slam me to the ground. Tarik glowed blood red before disappearing. "Remy, stop."

Without Tarik and the accompanying armor, fear washed over me, and I pressed my face into the ground.

Shit. I don't want to get shot. There's no one who'll be able to heal me. "Go back," I grunted at Unagi, knowing he'd get what I meant. I wanted to head back to the wall he'd been behind before he'd been forced to leave by my cavalier attitude. There we'd be relatively safe. I hoped.

Unagi's hot breath tickled my ear. "I'm going to roll off you in a second, then I want you to get to the wall while staying as low as possible. I'll be right behind you."

I may have been served up a healthy dose of fear when Tarik abandoned me, but I also didn't need Unagi to take care of me. I could handle myself. "You go first, I'll be behind you."

"Remy," he growled, muscles tensing around me.

"Then we can just lay here like this. It's kind of comfy, isn't it?" A bullet zinged past my ear, a bit too close.

Without another word, Unagi rolled off me, and started making his way towards the wall on all fours. Despite the situation, I couldn't help the grin that tugged my lips up. He knew I was stubborn to a fault. I couldn't help it, though; I'd been trained as the next Grand Witch of Domus Novem to protect my people, not the other way around. It didn't matter if I had no magic at my disposal, the instinct was still there.

Tiny stones and pieces of debris abraded my forearms, hands, and legs as I crawled across the ground. Once my head was behind the wall, Unagi jerked me up by my shoulders, dragging me the rest of the way to safety.

"Don't ever do—"

"No!" Owen's grief-stricken voice filled the air, everything else silencing.

Letting me go, Unagi peeked around the wall, me hot on his heels. There in the middle of everything was Owen, holding someone in his arms—or a part of them anyways. There was too much blood to tell what I was actually looking at.

"No, no, no!" Owen wailed. His body trembled before slumping over, blood seeping into his military fatigues. "God, please!" His voice cracked, breaking into sobs.

I pulled my gaze away, squeezing my eyes shut. It felt too personal—too raw. Whoever Owen was mourning had died violently, and suddenly. It reminded me too much of my sister. An image of her in Owen's arms appeared in my mind, wrenching a sob from me.

"Remy." Unagi's fingers slid down my cheek to catch a tear I didn't realize I'd shed. "Don't think about Callie."

I forced my eyes open, gazing up at him. "I just wanna —" All the color from the landscape leeched out of existence, leaving us in darkness once more. "Unagi?"

"I'm here."

Sunlight burst through the dark, illuminating a field filled to the brim with roses and neon trees. It was some sort of combination of the two dreamscapes I'd seen of Owen's so far.

"Hey. What were you sayin'?" Owen asked.

I glanced at him, then at Unagi, and back again. "Umm … What about—" Unagi elbowed me in the side, shutting me up.

"You don't remember?" Unagi addressed Owen while I rubbed my side and glared at his perfect profile.

"What you were sayin'? No."

Understanding dawned on me. The forests, the flowers, all the cheery, happy dreamscapes that Owen conjured ... when not having nightmares about things that had probably happened in real life. I wasn't a shrink or a dream analyzer, but I was willing to put money down that Owen had PTSD, and was probably in a coma. It would explain ... everything.

I heaved a sigh, trying to squelch the bitterness bubbling in my gut. Just my luck, the only human dreamer I'd come across, and he was broken. "Let's go," I muttered to Unagi. "We don't have time to waste on him."

"Mama!" Voo-Dolly burst out of the woods, tiny legs carrying her faster than I thought possible. "Kiernan needs you!"

Relief that Voo-Dolly was okay was quickly replaced by disbelief. "Is that where you were, with Kiernan?" I'd been beginning to think he really was dead. But instead, he was alive and kicking, and apparently trying to manipulate me by using Voo-Dolly. *Scheming asshat of a fae.*

"Yes, Mama." Voo-Dolly opened her arms to me. "Kiernan needs your help."

"My help?" I scoffed, bending down to scoop her up. "Please. That whole thing with the laruas was obviously a ploy. Boy, does he have the wrong witch if he thinks he can tug on my sympathy strings. Ha!" Kiernan claimed he knew me better than I knew myself from my dreams, but obviously not. You can't garner sympathy from someone who doesn't have any.

"Who's Kiernan?" Owen moved closer, his eyes riveted to Voo-Dolly.

I shifted her from one hip to the other, frowning. "A stupid fae. Trust me, you're better off not knowing who he is. I wish I didn't."

"Maybe we should see what he wants," Unagi muttered.

My mouth dropped open. "You can't be serious? After everything—"

"We're going to need help getting out of here, Remy. Surely you've figured that out by now. He's our best bet. Even if he is probably the reason why there aren't any other options."

"What about me?" Owen interjected. "I thought I was goin' to help you get out."

"Yeah, about that." I moved from foot to foot, petting Voo-Dolly as she pressed her face into my neck. "I think you're broken."

"Broken. What's that supposed to mean?"

"I think you're in a coma, which is why you can't figure out how to wake up."

Owen staggered back, his face going slack. "So that just means my way out will be a little harder to find, right?"

"You don't have a door," Voo-Dolly offered, not picking her head up. "I checked."

"What does that mean? That I don't have a door?"

I considered my words, but I wasn't known for my tact. "You're not going to wake up. Ever."

Owen paled, his baby blues glazing over. "So I'm dead or something? Or, I will be. Dead."

I was impressed by how well he was taking the news. I certainly wouldn't have. "No. When you die, you'll pass on. You'll stay here until that happens."

"So if I'm in a coma for ten years?" I raised my eyebrows. "Oh," he muttered, scrubbing a hand down his face. "So there's no chance?"

"Not if you don't have a door. Of course, Voo-Dolly could be wrong." I shrugged.

"She's not," Unagi said. "I don't sense a door either."

And that ultimately answered why he hadn't taken me to Owen before. It wouldn't have done any good. "Look, I'm sorry. But we have to go. We have to find a—"

"Wait! How do I move on? How do I … die?"

Unagi strode forward, his expression twisted with pity. He rested his hand on Owen's shoulder, squeezing. "Let go. Just let go. Sometimes that's the hardest thing, to let go of the life you wanted, the one you thought you would have. But it's already gone." He gave me a furtive glance. "And the sooner you let it go, the sooner you and all of your loved ones will find peace."

My heart constricted for some unknown reason, and I clutched at Voo-Dolly for comfort. "Mama, we have to go."

"Yes, I know."

The trees and flowers disappeared first, shimmering

out of existence, and then Owen faded, Unagi's hand falling to his side. He muttered something under his breath, too low to understand, before turning to me. "Come on. We have to find Kiernan."

I spared one last glance behind me at the empty space that had once held such beauty … and Owen, my heart roaring in my ears. *Get it together. What the hell is happening to you? You don't care about such things.* But it did no good. A lone tear trickled down my face and dropped off my chin.

I shuffled after Unagi, covering my sniffling with a series of coughs. I was pretty sure he knew what I was doing, and I was thankful he didn't call me out on it. Especially because I still had no explanation for why I was so sad all of a sudden.

Chapter 12

"That way." Voo-Dolly pointed to the right, and Unagi backpedaled a few steps to realign the direction he was heading in.

"Remind me again why you're trying to follow from the front. Voo-Dolly's the one who knows where we're going, not you."

"You can't follow from the front." Unagi tugged on one of the braids in his long white hair.

"Yes, you can. You've been doing it since we left the clearing. You're walking in front, pretending like you know where we're going, but you're relying on Voo-Dolly's directions. That's called following from the front."

"It's not," he grumbled, expression tense.

"You going to talk to me? Tell me what's bothering you?" My gaze traced the graceful lines of his profile, lingering on his supple lips. I rubbed at my mouth, thinking about how it would feel to kiss him. Ever since our moment in the woods, I hadn't been able to get him out of my head. It was beyond inconvenient, especially considering the circumstances. *But why can't a familiar and a witch have a sexual relationship? How perfect would that be?* I couldn't imagine intimacy on such a level. To have someone know me on every level possible—to be my true partner … No, I couldn't imagine it, but oh gods, I wanted it.

"No."

No? No, what? Oh yeah. "Familiars and their witches—"

"Should only be so close," he snapped, tugging harder on his braid.

"That's not true. Our kind of bond transcends—"

"Everything. And you need to stop thinking what you're thinking."

Of course he would know. "My thoughts are private, no one invited you!" Hadn't I just been wondering about sharing everything with someone? *Yeah, never mind.*

"There was once a male witch who fell in love with his familiar, a female werewolf."

"A werewolf?" I interrupted. "But that's—"

"As rare as a kitsune familiar, I know." Unagi squeezed my hand briefly before dropping it. "This was before it was … frowned upon to have relations with one's familiar. Of course it was still rare because most familiars can't take human form."

I nodded. I knew that. My sister's familiar had been a sprite. The thing hadn't been more than four or five inches tall. Magical beings were always drawn to be familiars, but not all of them were created equal. Usually, they were just needed to help out with small things, like channeling magic, mixing potions, or just being a companion, nothing major, most of the time.

"The witch and the werewolf formed a bond so tight that when she was killed, he went mad."

"Oh. And then I guess that's when the rule was made. Which isn't really a rule, it's more just a—"

"It's ingrained in every little witchling's mind that a relationship with their familiar is not acceptable because it keeps them safe, and the familiar, too. If we— If you would have— If we had that kind of relationship when you were murdered, for instance ..." His voice cracked and he paused to clear his throat. "If we had that kind of relationship when you were murdered who knows what I would have been driven to do to save you."

My heart sped up. "What happened to the witch, the one who went mad?"

"He killed a lot of people—witches, werewolves, humans—all before disappearing, never to be seen or heard from again."

Groaning, I shook my head. "Oh great. You know he's going to pop up again eventually to do all kinds of heinous things. Probably has a whole villainous plot laid out that he's just waiting for the right time to put into action."

Unagi threw his head back and laughed, the sound lifting my spirits. "This isn't a badly scripted movie, Rems."

Rems? I blinked up at Unagi, the way he shortened my name shook me to my very core, and I clutched at my chest. I'd thought when he'd said it before when he was waking up that he'd been slurring his words. The way he'd just said it, it was … it was—

"Rems?" I croaked. "Wha— Why? I feel like—" I stared hard at him as he froze in place, his breathing shallow. I grabbed at his wrist, just as he lurched to the side, out of my reach. "Show me your wrist." Things weren't adding up. There were too many inconsistencies, and all of them seemed to center around Unagi. "I said to show me your wrist!"

"I told you, it's not real."

"I want to see it anyways. Now." We stared each other down, neither of us moving.

Unagi's shoulders slumped. "Let it go."

My nails dug into my palms, my body quaking. Unagi's eyes were trying to tell me something he didn't want to have to say out loud. I thought back to the advice he gave Owen.

"Let go. Just let go. Sometimes that's the hardest thing, to let go of the life you wanted, the one you thought you would have. But it's already gone. And the sooner you let it go, the sooner you and all of your loved ones will find peace."

And he was saying it to me now. Let it go. But how could I let something go if I didn't know what it was? Were my memories more riddled from the laruas than I thought? But why wouldn't Unagi just tell me?

"Let what go?" I whispered.

"All of it."

Voo-Dolly, who'd been staring at us silently for the past few minutes, jumped at my legs, wrapping her arms around my calf. "Mama! Look!"

Unagi and I had fallen oblivious to our surroundings, not noticing when they'd dramatically changed. Instead of forest, we now stood in what could only be described as a dystopian setting. Dilapidated buildings served as the backdrop for overgrown pavement, complete with rusted cars. Very stereotypical. All it was missing was—

I groaned. "Zombies!" No less than a dozen of them shambled towards us, their decomposing corpses oozing things I didn't even want to consider. *Looks like the dreamer is going old school.*

"Great." Unagi rolled his eyes, mirroring my sentiments. "The vast majority of humans are very unimaginative."

"Well, you know, zombies are very popular with humans right now. At least we know how to kill them. I'd rather deal with stuff I know how to handle than new monsters who would rip us to shreds."

Unagi grabbed my arm and tugged me into his side. "Who said anything about killing? We run."

I shirked out from his grasp, a demonstrative pout forming on my face. "Oh, come on! I've always wanted to kill some real live zombies." I bounced in front of him, the pout stretching into a grin. "Call Tarik, please!"

"Rems—y, no. And besides, there's no such thing as real live zombies."

I narrowed my eyes at his use of Rems again, even though he'd tried to hastily play it off. I decided to ignore it. *One battle at a time.* "Please." I waved at the groaning zombies. "Look how slow they are."

Frowning, he tilted his head to study them. "It's a bad idea."

"Please!"

He crossed his arms over his chest. "Absolutely not."

"Tarik! Oh, Tarik! I don't know if you can hear me, but if you can, I know you want to help me kill some zooombies!"

"Rems, I said no."

"How many times do we have to have this conversation? You're not the boss. I am."

"That very well may be, but I won't call *my* sword." He raised his eyebrows defiantly.

"Stop being—"

With a bright flash of light, Tarik appeared in my right hand, glowing purple. It was a new shade for him, but I was going to take it as a good sign, like he was excited to help me kill some zombies. The magical armor flickered into place a moment later. "Ha!" I stuck my tongue out at Unagi, who looked like he was contemplating strangling me, and melting down his sword afterwards. "It'll be fine. I have armor and everything."

I skipped off towards the zombies, excitement causing me to practically vibrate. "This is going to be ah-maze-ing!" Tarik glowed a more vibrant shade of purple, obviously agreeing. It didn't matter if he affected my mood, I welcomed the reprieve from my constant muddled thoughts from being in Somniare.

The first zombie that reached me seemed a touch fresher than his companions, which was why he was a bit more agile, at least in comparison. He'd lost his shirt somewhere along the way, and I couldn't help but notice that he'd probably been quite good-looking when he was alive. *He was never alive. He was conjured by a human dreamer.* I laughed at my own ridiculousness and lunged forward, plunging Tarik into hot-zombie's chest.

"If these are traditional zombies, you have to get them in their heads," Unagi called.

"I know. Just having some fun first." I yanked Tarik out, danced back a few steps, and watched with fascination as hot-zombie's chest oozed black. *Ick. Maybe this isn't going to be as amazing as I thought.* Tarik quivered as if disagreeing with me. Either way, I was in for a pound.

"Yippee ki-yay, zombie bitches!" Feeling a bit whimsical, but also the need for high dramatics to maximize the good times, I spun in a wide circle, ending with Tarik's blade cutting through hot-zombie's flesh and bone like it was butter. The head thudded to the ground, and on a whim I punted it, laughing as the rotting stump sailed through the air like some kind of macabre soccer ball.

My antics upped the ante, and the rest of the zombie herd groaned with heightened agitation. *Maybe hot-zombie was popular with them?* I ran around to the back of the group, and while they struggled to turn with any kind of speed, I lopped off a few more heads, before racing back to stand in front of them again. I dropped down into a fighting stance and waited for them to converge on me.

They fanned out, hunting as a group, as if they were connected. I remained perfectly still until one by one they began to dive at me, teeth gnashing. The first I cleaved nearly in two down the middle, and the second I stabbed through her left eye before taking her head. By the third, I was bored and ready to end it. Much like the dance Tarik and I had performed to take down the laruas, I moved fluidly with him, never stopping, as I decapitated every last zombie. When all of the zombies were officially nothing but all-the-way-dead corpses, Tarik disappeared, taking the armor with him.

"Oh, gods!" I staggered to the ground, retching. Behind the protective barrier of the armor I hadn't been able to smell the rank odor of my attackers; without it, the rotting stench was like a punch to the face. I clawed at the slimy gravel, managing to get to my feet, staggering back to Unagi, who was looking a bit too smug.

"What?" I demanded.

His lips twitched. "Nothing." He waved his finger around, motioning to me. "You have a little …" His nose scrunched up in disdain.

I glanced down at my shirt and saw that I'd picked up a few souvenirs from my zombie buddies. "Ewwww!" I jumped up and down, trying to dislodge the gore without touching it.

"You're the one who wanted to play with the zombies. Bet you wish you would have listened to me now, huh?"

"Shut up."

Unagi rushed forward, reaching for me, his eyes flashing black. My throat constricted, pain lancing my skull just before everything went dark.

Chapter 13

"I'll rip your heart out with my bare hands," Unagi snarled. "I swear it!"

"Quite the overprotective familiar. A pity she doesn't know how protective. And why."

My head pounded, my eyelids weighing a ton each, but somehow I managed to peel them open. Adrenaline shot through my system when a masculine shape in dark robes came into focus. He stood over me, his hands extended, the dark golden glow of my magic racing from me to his palms and disappearing.

"Stop!" I grabbed at the air as if I could stuff it back into my body. "No, I'll die!" I wasn't sure why I was informing him of this, obviously he knew. After all, I recognized his voice from the ice-land nightmare.

He chuckled. "Unfortunate side effect, I'm afraid."

"Who are you?" Pain lanced my side, and I again

grabbed wildly at the air, my vision narrowing down to a sliver of light.

Somewhere a door slammed. Angry voices spoke; the words and meaning eluded me. Another door slammed. A rushing sound, kind of like the ocean, had taken up residence in my ears. My heart beat sluggishly, and I was cold. *So cold.*

I tried to focus, but everything was falling away.

"No, no, no, no, no." Hands as hot as the sun shoved under me, cradling my head. "Rems, please, you can't die now. Not after everything. Just hold on. Hold on just a little …"

I slid into darkness, finding peace. I drifted as light as the air, as carefree as—

I screamed, shooting straight up, potent magic flowing through my veins, scorching every molecule in my body. When the pain finally ebbed, and my vision cleared, I realized that Tarik was sticking out of my chest. I clutched at him, bewildered, and a little bit scared.

"Stop." Unagi slapped my hands away. "Let him finish."

Tarik's glow dulled and then faded before he slid from my flesh and clattered to the ground, lifeless. I immediately pressed my fingers over my chest, finding no wound. I raised my gaze to meet Unagi's. "What—"

He yanked me up, expression grave. "There's no time for explanations now. We have to get out of here before he returns."

"But … Tarik." I glanced at the ground to find that he was gone, a pile of grey dust all that was left.

"He gave his magic, his life to save yours. Don't waste it."

"What about you? Why—"

"I gave all I could give, but it wasn't enough. I would have died for you—gladly, just like Tarik, but even then I don't think I would have had enough." He yanked on my arm again, moving me towards a wall. "Now, you need to conjure a door out of here. Tarik's magic should have left you with enough surplus."

"Then why couldn't he have kept some for himself?"

"Rems, I'll explain later."

I nodded. "Okay. Okay." I lifted my hands, concentrating on a quick exit and a safe place, my brain still too fuzzy to drag up specifics. A large red door popped into existence, and I yanked it open. "Here goes." I intertwined my fingers with Unagi's and stepped through.

MUSIC BLARED—SOME pop song I didn't recognize. Feminine laughs intermingled with the music, making the air itself pulse with energy. I stood on the outskirts of a group of girls about my age, all of them dancing around in their pajamas.

"A sleepover dream, really?" I gave Unagi a sidelong glance, and then whipped my head back to do a double take. Gone was the original male version of my familiar, and in his place, wearing the same kimono sized to fit, was the original female version. I'd only seen her once before, and just like with the male version, it had ended with me having inappropriate thoughts.

I cleared my throat and shuffled my feet. "You changed. Does this mean you're almost back to normal with your magic levels?"

"I wish," she grumbled. "I still have a long way to go. That stupid cage nearly drained me completely." She turned her gaze to meet mine, the corners of her eyes crinkling. "Looks like you changed, too."

"Ah, man." I fisted the blue dress's skirt, hating that I was in the stupid thing again. "What the hell? Was it because I almost died? Did I revert somehow?"

Unagi's expression sobered. "Yes, exactly."

We fell into silence, both of us turning our attention back to the slumber party revelers. They seemed so happy, so carefree. I couldn't help but envy the human who was dreaming all of it. What kind of life does someone have that their slumber is filled with such simple joys?

A much easier one than mine.

My head and therefore my dreams were always filled with things I'd much rather forget most of the time. Being raised as the next Grand Witch of Domus Novem hadn't afforded me any latitude when it came to normal childhood things. Other than my sister, who I lost so young, I wasn't sure if I had any real friends, or if they were all trying to cozy up to me because of my house standing. I'd certainly never been to a sleepover where I stayed up all night giggling and talking about ... *Gods, what do you talk about at sleepovers?*

Unagi's warm hand slid into mine, holding it firmly, my skin humming pleasantly at the contact. "You have me. I'm your friend."

My chest constricted. Attraction aside, I thought it would be weird, or difficult for me to wrap my mind around Unagi being both male and female, and yet the same on the inside. But as I stood there, holding the female version of Unagi's hand, I realized I didn't feel any different than when the male version had been with me. Unagi's presence, no matter the gender, soothed and grounded me, making me feel connected to the world in ways I never had before. "You just met me. We can't be friends yet. Not really."

"This is why you never had friends." She squeezed my hand and pulled me into her side, moving her arm to my waist so I could rest my head on her shoulder. We were almost the same height when Unagi was female. "It's not because you were raised to be the Grand Witch, it's because you don't let people in. You have a wall around you all the time. That makes you a hard person to get to know." Her fingers danced along my hip, eliciting a shiver. "But I'm in your mind, Remy. You can't hide from me."

I turned my face into her neck, inhaling. Her scent was the same as the male Unagi's, except maybe a bit more flowery, and feminine. I threaded my fingers into her silky hair, tugging gently. She shifted into me, her grip tightening around my waist.

"You know," I whispered, "I think of you as *she* when you're like this, and *he* when you're the other original form ... or really I assign gender in my head to match whatever form you're in. But when you're the fox I don't know what to refer to you as. It seems wrong to think of you as an *it* when you're a fox." I swallowed, my throat dry. "Because you're so much more than just an *it* no matter what form you're in."

She chuckled. "Oh, Rems. Call and think of me however you wish, none of that matters."

My gut clenched, butterflies dive-bombing my stomach. I wanted this version of Unagi just as much as I wanted the male version. It twisted my insides because on one level they felt like different people, like I couldn't decide, but I knew they were the same. I was just attracted to Unagi's essence, I supposed. I wanted a connection to him or her any way I could get it because I craved more of the intimacy the relationship promised. *No wonder the male witch went mad when he lost his wolf.* I'd only known Unagi for a short period of time and already I couldn't imagine a life without my familiar.

Unagi pulled away from me reluctantly, her fingers trailing along the fabric of my dress. "You have to stop thinking of me like that. Please."

A lump formed in my already desert wasteland of a throat and I flicked my gaze away, inhaling her lingering scent. "I'm sorry. I guess I would rather focus on relationship drama or lack thereof than all the death stuff that's been tracking me."

Unagi stepped back into me, pressing her lips softly to

my cheek, right in front of my ear. "We'll make it through this, I promise."

She just stood there, her hot breath tickling the side of my face as laughter from the slumber party surrounded us in a warm cocoon. I could almost forget where we were and that I was hanging onto my quasi-life by a thread. For the moment, none of it seemed to matter. Or maybe it mattered more than ever since my death loomed over me like a constant shadow. Every second was precious, and potentially my last.

My heart quadrupled in speed, indecision paralyzing me. *I want to kiss her.* It was funny how when I was with the male Unagi, I willed him to take from me, for him to dominate, but now with the female Unagi, I wanted to be the one in control.

Screw it.

I turned into her, ensnaring her lips with mine. She tried to pull away, but I threaded my hands into her hair, holding her in place. With a soft whimper, her body molded to mine. I pushed my tongue into her mouth, entangling it with hers in a sensual dance. She tasted divine, like nectar of some kind, sweet.

"Mmm ..." I groaned.

Unagi ripped herself away from me, stumbling backwards. "We can't, please, Rems. We can't."

Instead of arguing, I opened my arms, inviting her back into my embrace. I'd thought before that male Unagi had implied his female side didn't want me. Now I was sure that was a lie. If Unagi thought staying away from me was the best course of action because something could happen to one of us … well, that was just ridiculous. Anything can happen to anyone at any time. Hell, a toilet seat could drop from the sky and flatten you at any moment. You can't live your life worrying about the bad stuff. You'll forget to live at all, suffocating with all the dark emotions.

Bright purple flashed and male Unagi stood in her place, a fierce expression tugging his face into harsh lines. "This can't happen, Remy."

I smiled. "You can only change between your two human original forms, huh? I can work with that." I stalked forward.

"Maybe the female side of me couldn't resist you, but I can."

I quirked an eyebrow. "And you made it seem like she was the one who didn't want me. Is it you then? Were you just trying to spare my feelings?" Although I was sure Unagi's male side wanted me, too, I needed him to talk to me about everything—to come clean about what was really bothering him.

He smirked. "Please. She wanted you the moment she laid eyes on you. First as a friend, a companion, and then more."

"And you?"

His lips pressed together in a thin line. "Just because I play the pronoun game, too, doesn't mean I actually think of myself as two separate beings."

"Then if you want me just as much as your female side, why? Just why?"

"We can't be, Remy. We just can't. It's too dangerous."

I wrapped my arms around my middle, like I was holding all of my emotions in. "Okay. Fine." But I didn't mean that, not really. I just knew that we had to move on from the subject ... for now. We couldn't stay in the slumber party dreamscape forever.

"Now would be a good time to fill me in on that male who was leeching my magic, and what happened to Tarik ... all of it. And I hope you have a plan for what's next, because I'm getting real tired of stumbling our way through one dreamscape to another without any idea what we're doing."

"Yeah, okay."

Chapter 14

U nagi explained what he knew as we ventured out of slumber party land, and back into the wild forest of Somniare. It was amazing how the tone of each dreamscape seeped into my psyche, coloring my emotions. While in the last dream, surrounded by laughter and lightheartedness, I'd felt much of the same on some level. That had quickly changed, though. Now my mood was plummeting towards rock bottom.

The male who had witch-napped me and been intent on sucking me dry of my magic, was a warlock. That's all Unagi knew for sure about him. His features were blurred by a cloaking spell, but the magical signature of a male witch gone rogue was unmistakable. Worse, the warlock seemed to know entirely too much about me and mine. Not just Unagi, but all of Domus Novem. I couldn't help but wonder if it was possible that he'd once been a male witch in our house.

There had been no signs of Kiernan since he'd pleaded for help, sending Voo-Dolly to fetch us. And now Voo-Dolly was missing again, lost somewhere between my zombie killing spree and my most recent near demise.

The longer I was in Somniare, the more complicated things got, and yet the only way for me to fix any of the problems was to get out of Somniare. *Talk about Catch-22.* Hell, I still had absolutely no clue who'd murdered me, which was issue number one in my book.

"Why does so much of Somniare resemble a forest?"

Unagi shrugged. "It's just the way it's always been. I'm sure there's a reason, I just don't know what it is."

I scanned a line of trees, the bunch of them looking identical to the group we just passed. "How do we know we're even getting anywhere?"

"We're eventually going to get somewhere."

"This entire place is made up from the fabric of dreaming, who's to say we'll ever get anywhere?"

"Are you going to ask me if we're there yet next, huh? Because your sudden doom and gloom attitude isn't helping anything."

I shot a death glare at the side of Unagi's head. "Yeah, well no one asked you to be here. I don't need your help. Or anyone else's for that matter."

"You'd be dead three or four times over if not for my help."

"Whatever." I started chewing on my thumbnail. "And what do we do when we run into more laruas or zombies now that we don't have Tarik?"

"He'll be back ... eventually."

I stopped dead in my tracks, mouth agape. "What? He's not dead, or destroyed? And you didn't mention that before because? Wait—" I waved my arms around frantically. "You mean he didn't give his life for me? Like you friggin' said?"

Unagi tugged at one of the braids in his hair. "He *did* give his life for you. But he has endless lives."

"Explain."

"He was forged in the fires of a phoenix. He will be reborn." Unagi grabbed my arm and tugged until I started walking again. "I just don't know how long it'll take."

"Why, becau—"

"Because he's never died before. Just because he has more than one life doesn't mean what he did was any less of a sacrifice."

"What about you? Do you have more than one life?"

"No."

"You know, you never did tell me why you decided to be my familiar out of the blue. Why now when you—"

"Why are you asking so many questions all of a sudden?" he snapped.

"Because I need answers!"

"Now isn't the time."

"Now is precisely the time when all we're doing is

walking in circles in the woods. I'd like to maybe know some of these things before the warlock pops up and finishes the job, or a gaggle of laruas swoop down to make me one of them." Heat built behind my eyes and I pressed my palms over them, rubbing. "Maybe I just want to get some stupid answers before I die."

I staggered, doubling over, gasping for breath. "I don't wanna die." Pressure released, and hot tears slid down my face.

The next moment I found myself in Unagi's arms as I sobbed. "Shhh ... It's okay. I won't let you die all the way. I'll never let that happen."

I was too hot, my skin too tight. I struggled to get away from him, swiping at my tears, sniffling. "Gods, this is embarrassing. I don't know what came over me."

Unagi scowled. "Don't do that. Don't be afraid to be vulnerable in front of me."

I stared at the ground, unable to lift my gaze. "It's not that—it's just that I don't feel vulnerable. I don't ... I don't know what came over me, really."

Unagi grabbed me by the shoulders roughly, the sudden movement forcing me to look up at him. "I'll tell you what came over you! Some of the things you've been stuffing down inside, the things you don't want to deal with, just bubbled to the service. It's natural for you to feel traumatized by all that's been happening to you."

"No. It's a weakness I can't afford. Not now, not ever. I've been trained to be the Grand Witch of Domus

Novem, and such useless emotions are something someone of my position can't afford."

"Emotions are never wasted, Remy, not as long as they're real. And everyone needs some outlet—someone to talk to."

I wiped my face one last time and rolled my eyes. "Okay, Mr. Confucius-says—emotions are never wasted. Yeah, whatever."

"Don't mock your own feelings."

"Don't tell me what I'm feeling!"

Unagi slammed against me, taking us to the ground, our lips and teeth clashing. I groaned when I tasted blood, the flavor of dull metal setting me on edge, heightening all of my senses. My skin ached, and Unagi's touch was almost painful, his hands roaming my body freely. I hitched my leg around his hip, arching up—

Unagi was half a dozen feet away. "Gods damnit!" He turned his heated lavender eyes onto me, the edges dabbled in gold. "This can't happen. Stop—"

"I didn't do anything this time!" I was done suffering whiplash from Unagi's mood swings with me. One minute he wanted me, and then he didn't. The next she wanted me, and then it couldn't happen.

"Yes, you did." He turned around, pressing his forehead into a tree. "Or maybe you didn't. I don't know what I'm doing with you anymore. I thought I had everything all figured out." He groaned, muttering, "I miss you so much it hurts."

"What? What does that even mean?" I stood slowly, my

knees a bit wobbly. "That's the kind of thing I'm talking about. I feel like you're hiding things from me. Tell me what they are."

"I can't. I just can't. I made a deal. I made a deal to save your life, Rems. And I can't tell you the horrible things I've done and been doing ever since. I couldn't bear the look in your eyes."

"Just tell me!"

"I can't."

My nostrils flared as I attempted to rein in my temper. It was no use though. "Fine. I'm doing this on my own from now on then. I want you gone. And when I get out of here—because I will, on my own—we're not bonding. I won't give you my mark because I can't trust you. Just like before I was murdered, I don't have a familiar."

Before he could protest, I rushed off into the woods, definitely, one-hundred- percent *not* crying again.

R.

A MOMENT *or two of weakness doesn't make a weak witch. A moment or two of weakness does not make a weak witch.*

I threw my head back and screamed, heat rushing through my body. Unagi got under my skin like no one or nothing ever had before. One minute I wanted to kiss him —or her—and the next I wanted to drill my fist into that beautiful face. Well, mostly the male version of him. *But am I being overly emotional?* Maybe Unagi wasn't the only one having mood swings. I was definitely all over the place when it came to our new relationship.

"You have a wall around you all the time. That makes you a hard person to get to know." Unagi's words echoed through my mind.

Were they true? Did I not have friends because I pushed everyone away? *Is that what I'm doing now with Unagi?* I mean, what had my familiar done that was so bad? I couldn't really expect Unagi to open up instantly to me either. Maybe I was being too harsh—maybe I was just trying to reject before I got rejected.

I turned around slowly, my gaze lingering on the path I'd just come from. *Maybe I should go back ... and apologize.* I waffled between stubbornness and forgiveness. There was no denying that Unagi was keeping secrets, but maybe it was best if I didn't know ... for now.

Screw it.

I trudged back the way I came, grumbling under my breath. *What if he doesn't accept my apology? What if—*

"Unagi!"

I scrambled into the clearing, my heart in my stomach. Unagi was lying on the ground, unconscious, as the warlock who'd witch-napped me before, encased him in a shadowy cloud of magic.

"Want him to stay in one piece? You'll come to me willingly. Be your little kitsune's hero." He chuckled before snapping, "I don't have time to chase you around anymore. You can buy his life with yours." He waved his hand, and a door opened, which he stepped through with Unagi floating behind him.

"Why do you want me?" *Is my magic that important to him?* He seemed powerful enough to me. Of course, warlocks were a power-hungry lot. *And why didn't he just throw down with me now? I'm right here.*

The warlock, the door, along with Unagi, disappeared into thin air. I dropped to my knees, my eyes bone dry— too dry. It was as if someone had sandblasted them.

My life for Unagi's?

No. I don't accept that choice.

I'd never understood the notion that sacrificing your life for someone automatically made you a hero. In my opinion, that would be the easy way out. I could just swagger into the warlock's humble abode, say a few snarky comments, and go out in a blaze of glory. I'd be remembered fondly—but ultimately my life would be over.

What kind of shit plan is that?

Finding a way to save Unagi, and live, now that would be a challenge worthy of being classified as a hero. Living was always the more difficult choice, no matter the situation.

But do I really want to be any kind of hero? I hated sticking my neck out for anyone. After all, being raised as a Novem had instilled me with a certain level of moral ambiguity. I wasn't a bad soul, but I wasn't necessarily good either. I could just as easily walk away from Unagi as—

Lie. Even as I tried to convince myself to walk away—to just worry about myself and get the hell out of Somniare—I knew I couldn't. No matter the issues between us, Unagi was mine.

And no one takes what's mine.

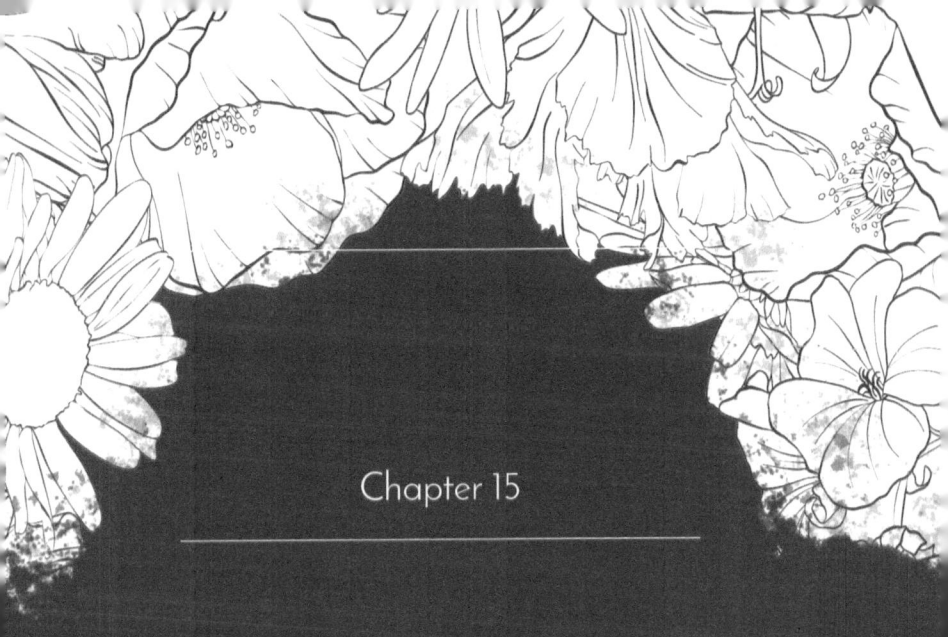

Chapter 15

The best-laid plans always go to crap.

Good thing I don't actually have a plan.

I picked right back up where Unagi and I had left off with the aimless wandering, and if I wasn't so damn stubborn, I would have been tempted to give up already. It was odd that I hadn't come across any new dreamscapes of any kind. It was just endless forest rolling into endless forest. No laruas either, so that was the upside.

But I felt so alone—alone in a way I never had before, which was disconcerting. After all, I had no true friends, and even in a crowd, I felt isolated on some level. It couldn't have had to do with missing Unagi's presence because the kitsune was a new addition to my world. Or maybe it had everything to do with Unagi because I'd been so desperate for attention I'd glommed onto the first bit I was shown. Since my sister died, I lived in darkness.

And if you live in nothing but darkness, the first bit of light becomes everything to you.

"Lost?"

"Kiernan?" I squeaked, spinning around in the direction his voice had come from. And sure enough, there he was in all of his leather-clad glory. "I never thought I'd ever be glad to see a fae!"

He pushed off the tree he'd been leaning against with utter casualness, his movements fluid like a panther stalking its prey. "Thanks for coming when I needed you." His voice dripped with sarcasm.

I stopped short, glaring. "Yeah, because you seem like you needed it." I demonstratively looked him up and down as if to say *'You look fine to me, no injuries.'* I clicked my tongue against the roof of my mouth. *So much for being glad to see his stupid fae-face.* Not that I'd ever actually seen his face ... which was weird. Most fae loved using their beauty as a weapon every chance they got.

"If I was anyone else I would have been dead. Instead, it merely took me longer to extradite myself from the rather sticky situation I'd gotten myself into."

"Mmm hmm. Yeah, okay ... whatever. You need to help me save Unagi."

Throwing his head back, he laughed. "And why would I do that?"

I bit my lower lip, fidgeting. I knew there was one thing that Kiernan had been trying to get from me since I'd arrived in Somniare. Could I give it to him for Unagi's sake? I didn't see any other options. I was officially desperate. "I'll give you my thanks."

Kiernan stilled. "You swear it?"

"Yes, if you help me get Unagi out in one piece—unharmed." I cleared my throat and sucked my teeth, reconsidering my words. I had to get them just right. "I will swear to give you my thanks only if you enable me to rescue Unagi, or rescue him yourself, getting him out of his life-threatening situation completely unharmed, and not handicapped magically in any way. I get him back whole, body, mind, and soul, or no thanks for you." I lifted my chin, staring into the shadows hiding Kiernan's face. "And if you double-cross me or Unagi in any way, I retain the right to not thank you."

"Deal."

"Just like that?"

He tilted his head. "Just like that."

It terrified me how much Kiernan wanted my thanks, but he really did seem to be my only option. "You going to give me a clue about what you're going to ask for, since we've entered into a bargain?"

"No." He waved his hand at me to follow him.

I shuffled after him reluctantly, hating that I was going to have to cooperate with him. "Remember when you said you had a lot to talk to me about? Are you going to—"

"The time for talking is over." He halted at the base of a large tree, waving his arm back and forth several times; his magic swirled to form a symbol in the bark. The bottom creaked open, revealing a set of stairs, which Kiernan rushed down immediately.

I hovered at the base of the tree, peering inside, my knuckles going white from gripping the edge of the opening. "Where are you taking me? I thought we were going to go get Unagi."

Kiernan's deep voice echoed up to meet my ears. "I need to track him."

"Can't you just figure out where he is the same way you find me all the time?"

"I'll need to track him differently." There was a loud clanging sound, which made me jump. "Get down here now if you want my help."

I swore under my breath, my entire body resisting the thought of having to go underground. Confined spaces of any kind freaked me out. *Yeah, look at me. The next big, bad Grand Witch of Domus Novem, totally claustrophobic.* I took one tentative step after another, pressing my hands into the wall, fighting the urge to turn around and run away.

"You could use some more light down here." No response came. "You really are an ass—" Pain tore through my skull, and when I clutched at my temples I lost my balance and tumbled forward.

Kiernan caught me in mid-flight before I had the chance to break my neck. "Tell me what's wrong."

"M-my head," I gritted out between clenched teeth. "It's—"

Suddenly I was somewhere new, but I also sensed I was still in Kiernan's arms, his hold strong around me.

My gaze focused in on the spelled warlock, who was standing over Unagi, hands moving to manipulate the grey, shadowy mass encasing my familiar. Unagi's eyes were squeezed shut, tears running down his swollen cheeks, and his mouth was open in a silent scream as he writhed in agony on the stone floor.

"Tell me what I want to know and it can stop. The pain will stop."

Unagi thumped his fists against the ground, snarling, "I-I'm going to kill you. I'm going to kill you for hurting her."

The warlock laughed. "I was kind of hoping you'd say that."

Unagi's scream ricocheted in my head as I blinked Kiernan back into focus. I grabbed at him, clawing the sides of his leather hood. "He's torturing Unagi! We have to hurry!"

Kiernan set me down gently, his hands running up my back and across my shoulders, pulling away from me much too slowly for my taste. "You shouldn't have that kind of bond with him ... yet."

"Yeah, well I do. A lot of things are wonky here in Somniare." I started pacing, my gaze flitting around the small room we were in. It was barren except for a bed. *Of friggin' course.* What the hell had that clanging sound been? Did he conjure the bed out of thin air just to be an ass? "What is this place? Why are we here?"

"Calm down. It may take some time to track him."

"And what, in the meantime you want me to get comfy

in your little bed? Preferably naked, right?" I bit at my nails, nervous energy fizzing through my blood. *I need to get to Unagi. He's suffering because of me.*

"I won't stop you if you being naked is what you desire."

I put my hands on my hips and shot daggers at him with my eyes. "Ha! Not happenin', buddy. Now tell me why you seem to be able to pop up everywhere I am, but tracking Unagi is," I raised my hands to form air quotes, "going to take time?"

"Because I haven't had his blood," Kiernan growled, throwing his hood back.

I scurried away, the backs of my knees hitting the bed, where I landed in a heap. "You're ... you're—"

"Go ahead and say it!"

"Goblin! You're a goblin!"

My mind reeled with the implications. No wonder he'd made sure I'd never seen his face. He was quite happy letting me think of him as one of the light fae, and not what he actually was—one of the darkest of the dark fae. Now his words finally made sense to me.

"Would it be so bad to be with someone like me?"

It's why he lacked so much of the arrogant light fae attitude. Goblins, although powerful, were looked down upon in the fae hierarchy. Hell, they were feared and snubbed by all magical beings, witches included. But it wasn't their appearance that made them so terrifying. In fact, as my gaze roamed over Kiernan, I couldn't help but be drawn to his beauty, just like with his light fae cousins.

His features were finely made, elegant even—his jaw strong, and his cheekbones high. But no luminescent, golden skin, and no jewel-toned eyes for him. Instead, he had ice-blue eyes so light that they appeared almost white, and his skin was metallic silver. His hair was long, and jet-black, pulled into a leather thong at the base of his neck. No, it wasn't what goblins looked like that terrified everyone, but the type of magic they wielded. Dark magic. Which meant—

Shit.

"You've been feeding me black magic!" I brought a trembling hand up to cover my mouth. No wonder I was the strongest witch in Domus Novem. Black magic was easier to control and stronger. It's why so many witches, once they tasted it, fell under its addictive thrall. "You've tainted me!"

Kiernan bared his teeth, exposing fangs. "Don't be a close-minded *cailleach,* so set in your narrow views of magic. Nothing has changed about you except that you now know where your heightened power comes from."

"Yeah, the dark side of magic. I'm a tenebris witch! How didn't I sense it? How did no one else?" I stood, anger overcoming my fear just like it usually did. *Because I'm a tenebris witch? Being morally ambiguous, playing in the grey of magic was one thing ... but black magic? Nope. Nope. Nope. I'd lose myself eventually, the sludge of the black magic eating my soul.*

"You sampled my blood so you could track me. When?" If I'd known he was a goblin I would have known right away how he was tracking me, and I wouldn't have needed to ask. Once a goblin tasted your blood, he or she could find you anywhere … forever. *As if owing him a favor isn't bad enough. Now I know he's linked to me by way of blood until the day I die.*

"Why does it matter? I had so many opportunities with you bleeding all over Somniare."

"You played me. You played me for a—"

"Hush!" he roared. "Nothing has changed. Nothing. Black magic isn't dirty like its name implies. It's the intent of the practitioner using it that makes the difference."

We stared at each other, gazes locked in a battle of wills. Then my mind flashed to Unagi. Heaving a sigh, I looked away. Kiernan was right. Nothing had changed. I still needed his help to save Unagi.

"All right. Fine. I guess it doesn't matter anyways since I never liked you to begin with."

"Stupid, *cailleach*," he muttered, a faint smile twisting up one side of his mouth.

"But you are going to talk—spill it all after we save Unagi."

"No, I'm not."

"Uh, yeah, you are."

"We'll see."

Why did I feel like he'd said that just to shut me up? *Dumbass goblin.* I flopped on the bed, and waited, although not very patiently.

Chapter 16

"What exactly is taking so long?" I rolled over onto my stomach, glaring at Kiernan's muscular back. He'd been toiling over a small caldron, for what seemed like hours, muttering in another language under his breath. It had to be some goblin-ish tongue since my rune didn't translate it for me.

"I don't want to merely track Unagi, but to do it so that Jared doesn't know we're coming."

I perked up. "You know how to do that? Track completely undetected?" I knew it was possible, but I'd never learned the magic. "And Jared is the warlock's name? Do you also know what house he's originally from? Or anything about him?"

He grunted something nonsensical; his focus on what he was doing unwavering.

"What are you doing here in Somniare to begin with?" It was unheard of for goblins to be without their troops, which was their equivalent to domos magicae. Light fae, especially if they weren't interested in all that glittered in the royal courts, tended to be solitary creatures, unless mated, which was rare. I guess forever takes on a whole different meaning when you actually can live for that long. "When did you get here?" I nibbled on my thumbnail, kicking my feet up in the air behind me. "And why—"

"Do you want me to track Unagi or not?" Kiernan growled, his accent thicker. "Because all of your questions are not helping me to concentrate."

I hung my head, suddenly feeling like I was five again. "Sorry."

"Do you want to learn?"

I flicked my gaze back up to see he'd turned towards me, his ice eyes studying me. "Learn what?"

"How to track undetected."

I narrowed my eyes, wondering what the catch was. No fae, goblins included, liked to share knowledge without a price. Of course, Kiernan was already going to get what he wanted from me ... my thanks. I shrugged, feigning nonchalance. "Sure, why not?"

"Then come here."

"Is this going to make it take longer? Because we need to get to Unagi—"

"I wouldn't worry too much about your kitsune. Jared

won't harm him beyond repair as long as he has to use him as leverage."

"He's still in pain. I saw—"

"But you haven't seen anything else, which means Jared is probably leaving him alone for now. You aren't his primary focus. He merely wants your magic."

"How do you know so much about this Jared?"

Kiernan shifted into a crouch, picking up a small scrap of paper from the floor. "He was the cause of my sticky situation. While he was attempting to steal my magic," Kiernan chuckled, "as if his meager warlock powers were a match for mine, he left his mind vulnerable for me to slide into. I learned a lot about our new friend."

"Why were you in trouble if his magic is no match for yours?"

"I was taken by surprise, and when that happens, the stronger doesn't always win. Fortunately, I am goblin, and—"

"Nearly impossible to kill. I've heard." Rolling off the bed, I approached Kiernan slowly, my heart doubling in speed. I came to stand behind him, and I shifted so I could peer over his shoulder. His scent surrounded me, the spicy aroma intoxicating, different from before. "I should have known you weren't light fae, but your scent was—"

"I masked my scent. Made it so you smelled what you expected."

"Of course you did." Goblins were more slippery than the trickiest of their lighter cousins, but I'd never actually seen a goblin in real life. Fae, especially of the royal court variety, were definitely something I was familiar with. I'd even had a crush on one when I was about twelve. The stupid fae had enjoyed antagonizing me.

"So, are you going to show me what you've been doing over here?" I reached out to touch his shoulder but stopped myself short.

Kiernan stood abruptly, his icy eyes fierce as he blew a cloud of black dust into my face. I choked on it, eyes, nose, and mouth burning. "Wh-what are you doing?"

"This is the best way."

I collapsed, everything going dark.

R.

I SAT UP, fully aware, my pulse racing. *Where the hell am I?* I staggered to my feet, spinning in a circle. Green—green in every direction. But not trees, it was a hedge, or one large, unending hedge. I realized that I was at the entrance of some kind of maze. "Damnit! I knew I shouldn't trust him!"

But why had he sent me here? If he wanted my thanks so much, then why would he break our deal? Fae could be depended on if a proper deal was struck, and it had been, at least I thought so. We'd only verbally agreed, which held power, but we hadn't sealed it in blood, which maybe should have been a tip-off. So what had been Kiernan's angle—for any of it?

"Mama!" Voo-Dolly appeared out of thin air.

I scooped her up into my arms. "I'd thought you were gone for good." I hugged her tightly, thoughts turning briefly to my sister. "What's going on? How did you get here?" If Kiernan had sent her, too, her presence couldn't be trusted.

"I don't know. I've been looking for you everywhere." Her burlap face was rough against my neck as she rubbed it back and forth.

My vision tilted, everything blurring for a moment. When everything crystallized, I tried to remember what exactly I was doing, but minor details eluded me. *How did I get here? Where's Kiernan? Where did—*

"Remy! Come on!" Unagi in fox form stood at the edge of the maze. "Hurry!" Tails whirling in a circle, Unagi dashed off, clearly expecting me to follow.

I blinked, confusion causing me to falter. *Unagi was missing, right? No. That's not exactly— No, I can't remember.* "Unagi, wait!" I hurried into the maze in search of my familiar. "Something's wrong with all of this!"

"It's Somniare, Mama," Voo-Dolly said.

And that was very true. Nothing had been quite right since the moment I'd landed in Somniare. I set Voo-Dolly down, letting my gut guide me. I didn't get more than a half dozen-yards into the maze when I saw the end of Unagi's three tails, and I made a sharp right to follow.

"You don't deserve to live! Your sister was the special one! Not you!" My mother loomed in front of me, dressed as if to go to my ascension ceremony. "I'm the one who killed you. I couldn't pretend anymore."

I shook my head. "No. No, this isn't real."

"Maybe me being here in Somniare isn't the truth, but I can tell you what is—I never loved you. I merely suffered you to live because you were destined to be the next Grand Witch. But then I couldn't stand the thought of you holding such a position of power so I killed you."

Was I seeing my mother again, having another nightmare of her hatred for me because that's how I felt deep down? That she hated me? I'd thought I'd hidden away all my feelings of insecurity so deep that even I'd never find them again … obviously I'd been wrong. *I need to somehow overcome this.*

Wrapping my arms around my middle, I forced my gaze to meet my mother's. "You loved me. Maybe not as much as Callie, but you still loved me. You would never kill—"

"No. I never loved you because you're unlovable."

A lump formed in my throat. *Stop it. Just stop it. How old are you? Grow up and stop letting your* mommy *affect you. It's not even really her.* "I am lovable."

She laughed, doubling over. "No one is ever going to love you."

Pressure built behind my eyes, and my face heated. "Shut up! I'm—" I swallowed my words. "You know what? It doesn't matter what you think. Not anymore. Even if you never loved me, it doesn't mean I'm unlovable. I am."

My mother's image shimmered and disappeared,

clearing the path. I rolled my eyes. "Really? I stabbed her in the other nightmare, but that wasn't good enough? I had to tell her I'm lovable?" Or did I have to believe it myself? Why? *Hell, I'm not a psychologist and I don't have time for this. I need to get out of here.*

"Remy, this way!" Unagi called, and I followed the sound of its multi-layered fox voice.

As I rounded the next corner of the maze, my foot slipped in a pool of blood, and I hit the ground hard, biting my tongue. Something whizzed past my ear, cold as ice. I slapped at it, missing.

"Remy!"

I pushed myself up, warm blood dripping down my arms and legs, my dress heavy with it. I gasped when I saw the pathway ahead of me. There lay my sister's lifeless body, surrounded by the entire Domus Novem. Hundreds of them, their bodies stacked high; dull, lifeless eyes all trained on me.

"Remy!" I glanced around wildly, but no one spoke, no one was alive to say anything. "You let this happen! You weren't strong enough of a Grand Witch! This is your fault."

One-by-one the bodies shuddered and moved, ambling to their feet. I was paralyzed with panic as they started shuffling towards me, arms outstretched. They weren't zombies, not really, but they were close enough. "No! I didn't do anything!"

"Exactly. You didn't do *anything*!"

For a moment, when I'd faced my mother, I'd

considered the possibility the maze would be filled with things that had traumatized me, some of my fears, that type of thing. The dreamer who conjured up the maze had stolen the concept, just like the field of murderous flowers. But this—this didn't feel like that anymore at all.

I backed away slowly, glancing over my shoulder to see Voo-Dolly waiting for me. "Mama! This way!"

Laughter, dark and foreboding surrounded me, closing me in a cloak of dread. In one direction was a horde of very pissed-off dead witches, and in the other, Voo-Dolly, a creature who I didn't know the origins of. Sure, I kept telling myself that she'd been sent by my sister from the beyond, but I had no proof of that. Maybe she'd been made by Kiernan to steer me through Somniare in the directions he wanted. She could have been one massive tool of manipulation. Hell, for all I knew, Unagi wasn't real either. I couldn't trust anything, could I? Not even my own instincts. I was drowning in a sea of uncertainty, unable to decide which direction to go.

"I'm real. Never doubt our connection, no matter what happens. Trust your instincts. You know what's true and what's not, deep inside." Unagi's female voice rolled through my mind.

She's right. Even if I can't use my magic, it's still inside of me. I can't turn my back on it or it will turn on me. That was another lesson that had been drummed into my head since I was a small child. *'If you don't trust in your magic, if you turn away from it, it will turn from you.'*

I squeezed my eyes shut, spinning slowly in a circle

while searching my intuition. I tried not to hear the heavy-balled footsteps of the living-dead, or Voo-Dolly calling for me. The sounds bled together after a few seconds, and I stopped, smiling to myself.

I know what to do.

I lifted my skirt, twisting and pulling it through and around my legs, tying it up until it resembled shorts. I then scrambled towards the hedge in front of me, pulling myself up. *Why thank you, yes, I'll choose secret door number three.* I wasn't going to face off with the dead witches or follow Voo-Dolly.

"Mama!" she called, her tone dejected.

My heart squeezed. "Meet me at the end of the maze. Stay safe."

She nodded, seeming mollified. "Okay, Mama. I love you!" She scampered off without another word.

I really need to figure out where she came from so I can know whether or not to trust her.

Clammy fingers dug into my ankle, and I kicked out. My foot made contact with something solid, and a crunching noise made me cringe, followed by a low moan. I was already about halfway up the hedge, but climbing the thing was more difficult than I expected. The higher I got, the more I sank into it, the twisted branches getting smaller and smaller, and less able to hold my weight.

"Take my hand!" A teenage boy's face peered at me from the top of the hedge, his arm outstretched.

I hesitated for only a moment before I grabbed his offering, letting him hoist me up the rest of the way. By the time I made it to the top, I was sweating, and my muscles were trembling from the exertion. "Tha—" I stopped myself short, almost having thanked the boy. *Stupid, stupid, stupid.* "Wow. That was close." I shifted uneasily, half expecting to fall through the top of the hedge, but surprisingly it was as solid as the ground.

"Getting up here is the hard part. But once you're up, it's smooth sailing."

From my new vantage point, I could see the maze we were in went on as far as the eyes could see—possibly unending. Despite the situation, my entire body tingled with anticipation. *Finally, another human dreamer.* "How do we get out of here? Since you seem like an expert." *Wait.* There was something I had to do first. Someone I needed —missed. I pressed my fingers into my temples, rubbing. *Focus on the now. You need this dreamer.*

"We don't, get out that is. Or maybe I just haven't figured it out ... yet."

I studied the boy as his attention shifted to the maze, frustration twisting his expression. He was tall, lanky, and about my age, if not a tad older. His disheveled dark hair, which came to about his chin, framed a handsome face, where wire-rim glasses perched on his strong nose. He wore a dark blue flannel and baggy jeans. He was kind of cute in a nerdy-grunge way.

"How long have you been up here?"

"I'm not sure. A while, I think."

Great. He was probably another Owen, with no way

out of Somniare. "Do you remember where you were or what you were doing right before you came here?"

"Yeah," he spat. "I was protecting my mom from my step-father, not that she ever appreciated it." He turned his brown eyes on me, his expression stark. "We're in hell, aren't we? The bastard beat me to death and yet I somehow ended up here? I knew life was a bitch, but I had no idea the afterlife would be, too."

I touched his arm gently. "No, we're not in hell. We're in a place called Somniare. It's a place of dreaming."

"Dreaming?" he scoffed. "More like nightmares."

"Yeah, well that, too." I glanced down at the hundreds of living-dead who were still reaching for me, their lifeless eyes managing to portray hatred somehow.

He chuckled. "Yeah, I've been watching you since you came in here. If those things all came from your head, you're as broken as I am."

I jerked away. "I'm not broken. I'm a witch. Things are different for my kind than yours."

He nodded, his lips twitching. "Mmm hmm, definitely broken. But hey, I've seen other people come through here, and you're the first I cared enough about to help. So being broken helped you out because you're broken like me. Messed up family life and all."

I stilled, considering his words. I couldn't quite remember how I'd gotten to the maze, and I was positive I was forgetting more than a few very important details, but I couldn't shake the feeling that this boy was going to be important to me. *Yeah, like maybe he's finally my ticket out of Somniare.*

Grabbing his hand, I intertwined my fingers with his. "Come on. Let's figure a way out of here." I yanked him forward, walking with determination, even though I had no idea where I was going.

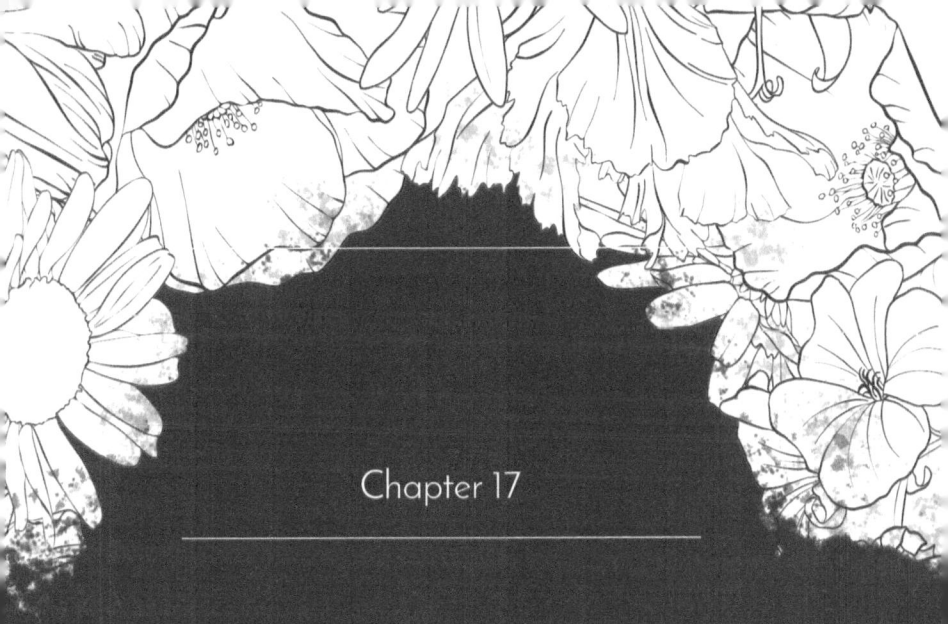

Chapter 17

"A witch, huh? You know those aren't real, right?" Miles smirked while peering at me from the corner of his eye.

I sighed. I'd gone the same route as I had with Owen, explaining that I was a witch and I merely wanted to hitch a ride out of Somniare … blah, blah, blah. The difference was that Miles was a vivid skeptic. He was convinced I'd lost my mind, but it was okay because I was cute. I simultaneously wanted to punch and thank him for the latter part. The good news was that either way he seemed okay with me hitching a ride. *Score!*

"I'm not crazy. I *am* a witch."

"You've just been here too long. All the messed up stuff in this place has eroded your brain. I mean, I thought I was in hell. It'll be okay though … once we get out of here."

His hand was warm in mine, reassuring, making me

think of Unagi. *Where is that damn fox anyways?* I squinted, a dull throb starting behind my eyes. "Explain how—"

"Being in a dreamscape pretty much explains everything."

Laughing, I rolled my eyes. "Yeah, I guess it does." I liked Miles. Although I wasn't attracted to him, he was … nice, funny even. I found myself being entertained by his dry wit. I'd never actually spent time with a human before. It turned out they weren't that bad, or at least Miles was representing his race very well. I guess I just assumed all humans were like the sketchy dregs who purchased spells from Domus Novem.

Miles stopped short, scanning the top of the maze. "I think … I think we should go this way." He raised the hand holding mine, so we were both pointing to the left.

"You sure?"

"You said to picture the outside world—home." He swallowed, his Adam's apple dancing in his throat. "And when I do, I feel this tug." He nodded once firmly. "Yes, I'm sure we need to go this way."

The tiny hairs on the back of my neck rose, prickling with awareness, as if I was being watched. I tugged my hand out of Miles' and turned, scanning our surroundings. *Nothing.* I couldn't shake the uneasiness, though, and even after we started walking again, I fought the urge to break into a run.

Stop being paranoid.

But it's Somniare, it's not paranoia, it's called being prepared.

I huffed, knowing that both points I'd made with myself were true. There was a fine line between being prepared and paranoia in Somniare, and I wasn't sure I knew what that line was anymore.

"What is it?"

"I don't know. I just feel like I'm being watched." I nibbled on my bottom lip before moving on to bite at my thumbnail. We came to another fork in the hedge, and I nodded back and forth between both directions. "Which way?"

"What the hell is that?"

My eyes stretched wide as a cloud of bugs descended upon us, their buzzing wings drowning out my response to Miles. "Run!" But he seemed to get the sentiment when I yanked on his arm.

We sprinted forward, me in the lead even though I didn't know where we were going. The bugs, which looked like some kind of super mutant locusts, ignored us and went straight into the hedge, their tiny mouths devouring everything in sight, ripping and chewing like starved hyenas.

And that's when I knew—they'd come to remove our sanctuary. We couldn't hide on the top of the maze anymore if there was no more hedge. We'd be fair game then. Miles must have come to the same conclusion right around the time I did because he picked up the pace, surging in front of me.

The wind whipped, making it difficult to see with the scraps of leaves and twigs hitting me in the face. I swore under my breath, wishing I could use my magic. Miles tripped, face-planting in front of me, causing me to get tangled up in his legs and land on his back.

I scrambled to my feet, tugging him to his. "Come on!" I screamed.

Grimacing, he picked a bug from the front of his glasses and tossed it aside, a dark smudge left in the middle of the lens. He blinked a few times, as if processing things, and then took off at a dead sprint. I was close on his heels, praying he wouldn't fall again, or I wouldn't for that matter. We were about to be up the creek without a paddle as soon as the bugs finished their mid-day snack. Behind me, a loud crash sounded, but I refused to look back, it would only slow us down ... or freak me out, neither being productive to our escape.

My foot dangled, hanging in mid-air for a moment, as I belatedly realized my path had disintegrated right before my eyes. I pin-wheeled my arms, trying to put myself in reverse, but it was too late. The wind ate my scream as I plummeted to the ground.

Several of the living-dead clamored to grab me, having been lying in wait. I kicked frantically, their hands sliding from my ankles as I crab-walked backwards, them too close for me to manage to get to my feet. *Where is Miles? I'm going to be so pissed if he leaves Somniare without me.*

My skin hummed with magic a moment before something appeared in my right hand. I curled my fingers around it, sensing immediately what, or rather *who* it was. "Tarik! You're back!" He glowed purple, obviously ready for action. Sparks of indigo flame zinged off the blade, tunneling into my flesh. I felt no pain … only clarity.

Unagi.

I didn't wonder how I'd forgotten. I knew. *Kiernan.* The question was: why? And I would be finding out, just as soon as I kicked some living-dead ass.

Tarik's mood uplift was welcome, especially compared to the near panic I'd been feeling moments before his arrival. It was kind of like downing a couple cups of coffee; I felt like I could take on the world, and do it with pizzazz.

Bursting with giddiness, I jumped to my feet and removed two living-dead witches' heads in one elegant sweep of my arm, their useless flesh thumbing to the ground. Unlike with the zombies, I didn't take the time to study them. Even though they were mere facsimiles of Domus Novem witches, the reanimated corpses still looked like my family, and I didn't want the images of me slaughtering them burned into my already messed-up psyche. Instead, I forced my gaze to blur, focusing only on movement, not features, letting Tarik guide me, which he was more than happy to do.

"Remy!" The deathly voices rose in unison, scolding and pleading at the same time. I ignored them, continuing to plow down body after body, soothed by the rhythm of thud after thud. "You did this to us!"

"Shut up," I hissed. "Just shut up."

"Remy!" I sucked in a sharp breath, spinning towards the new voice behind me on instinct. Tarik tugged, resisting the movement for some reason, but I forced my hand, jabbing the katana straight into—

"No!"

"Nice ... moves." Miles collapsed backwards, his legs crumpling awkwardly underneath him.

I glanced over my shoulder, just to make sure I wouldn't be attacked from behind, before dropping to my knees beside him. I waved my hands uselessly in the air, unsure of what to do. Tarik was embedded in Miles' stomach, glowing a shade of sickly yellow. "Oh, gods, Miles, I'm sorry—so sorry. I thought you were another one of them."

His lips twitched into a small smile. "No worries. I should have known better than to walk up behind someone wielding a glowing katana while battling zombies."

I sputtered on a laugh. "You'll be fine. Tarik can heal you ... right, Tarik?" I stroked my fingers over the hilt, hoping for some kind of sign. And I got one. Tarik flickered between yellow and red before popping out of existence. *Guess that means he won't be any help.* My heart dropped to my feet.

"It's okay." Miles coughed, blood oozing from his wound and the corner of his mouth. "It doesn't hurt." He coughed again, the sound wet, and gurgling. "I guess I'm in shock."

Belatedly I went into action, pressing down on the puncture wound. "I don't think I hit any major organs. If I can find something to stitch you up with—"

Miles placed one bloody hand over mine, squeezing gently. The scent of decay and rusty metal mingled in the air. "I think I'm ready to die. Maybe I'll find some kind of peace ... finally."

"No. This isn't right. You're a dreamer—this shouldn't be able to happen to you. You can't die in Somniare!"

As I gathered magic in my hands, the energy pulsing in my palms, I told myself that I wanted to heal Miles because he was my ticket out of Somniare, but I knew it was a lie. Over the short period of time we'd spent together, I'd learned about him. He'd opened up to me and shared the torrid details of his short existence in a way that no one ever had before. *It's funny how someone can become a friend almost instantly and others remain strangers no matter how long you know them.* Miles' life hadn't been an easy one, and I wanted—no *needed* to give him a second chance.

I'd always thought of myself as morally ambiguous—selfish to the core. The witch standing over Miles, ready to heal him at a personal loss, was not one that I recognized. But I think I liked her ... just a bit. Even if she was a big-time idiot.

My magic poured into Miles, filling and mending, making him whole. It was exhilarating knowing that maybe he would make something of the second chance I would give him. I just hoped I wouldn't end up dead. I prayed I had just enough energy in surplus to make it all work. *Just once let me have my cake and eat it, too. Please.*

That place of intuition inside me jolted with the

knowledge that he was healed, and I clamped down on my flow of magic like I was turning off a faucet, immediately looking down at my dress to assess the damage I'd done to myself. Before I could take stock, I rose off the ground, my hair whipping into my face.

"Remy, wh-what's happening?" Miles murmured, his voice a bit dazed.

As if an invisible hand tossed me through the air, I hurtled through Somniare, colors blurring before my eyes. Then I was falling … falling, falling, falling.

But none of it mattered. For just a moment I let myself revel in my selfless deed. *Whatever happens later, I saved Miles … just because.*

Chapter 18

"Well, that was quite a ride ... all of it!" Miles' face appeared over mine, his glasses glinting in the dim light. "I may be willing to reconsider my stance on you being a witch, by the way." He grinned.

I sat up slowly, shaking the disorientation from my foggy brain. "Still alive—or quasi-alive," I muttered, letting my hands skim over my side. *No blood.*

"This is the first time I've been out of that maze since I came here." He patted my arm, his excitement palpable.

I, however, didn't share his enthusiasm. "Great. Right back where I started." The huge trees of the main part of Somniare loomed over us. *How the hell did we end up here? And where is Kiernan? I know he has to be lurking nearby somewhere. This whole thing has the stench of him all over it.*

I stood, dusting myself off, leaving my dress tied up

between my legs. It was kind of ingenious, and I wanted to kick myself for not thinking to do it sooner.

"Enough with the games, Kiernan. Show yourself." Wind whipped around me, and my nose itched with the scent of his wild magic. "Stop being so damn dramatic and show yourself!"

"I'm not the dramatic one," Kiernan said, his voice carrying on the wind even though I still couldn't see him. "Brought you a present."

"Mama!" Voo-Dolly ran at me, throwing herself into my arms.

I stiffened. "Did you create her? No more lies." He'd told me to toss her away when he'd first seen her, but of course that could have been an act, knowing I'd probably do the opposite.

"No. You did." Kiernan appeared behind Miles, arms crossed, leather hood covering his face. Miles scrambled away, eyes as big as saucers. Kiernan ignored him. "When you shattered the glass with your magic, freeing Unagi from the nightmare, you leaked more energy than you thought."

I remembered the incident in question, and it was ... possible. My heart sank. She wasn't from my sister. I wiggled a pin that jutted out of Voo-Dolly's leg. "It's why she calls me Mama." Why had I ignored that before? It was so simple, so telling. *Occam's razor.* I guess I wanted to believe she was from my sister so I ... believed. I'd chalked up the whole mama thing to the fact that I'd made the original doll with my own two hands. *Looks like I made the second one, too.*

"Come," Kiernan commanded.

"I don't think so. We had a deal, and I don't know why you sent me to—"

He waved his hand, several laruas appearing behind him. They hovered, their dark shapes pulsing with hunger. "You can control them?" It was a stupid question, since he obviously was, but I was confused. It was like what I was seeing wasn't processing fully, or I didn't want it to.

"But of course, I hold dominion over Somniare and all in it."

My lips parted in shock. I'd been a fool—a young, naïve fool. "Has anything you've told me been the truth?"

"Omissions aren't lies." He pointed at Miles, and the laruas swarmed him.

"No!" I raised my palms, ready to blast them, but Kiernan wrapped his arms around me. I struggled, but I might as well have been bound by steel, all the progress I made.

His breath heated my cheek as he whispered in my ear, "Don't worry, I'm merely keeping him for later."

"But I saved him." I bit at Kiernan, the taste of leather bitter in my mouth, his choice of clothing serving as armor against me. I pulled magic into my hands, but I sensed he was binding my energy, controlling the powers that he himself had strengthened in me. "Why? Why are you doing this?"

My heart shattered, and my throat constricted, my gaze riveted on the sight of the laruas feeding on Miles. I barely blinked, barely breathed as Miles' form faded, the laruas stealing his memories—until he was no more.

The air shifted, cooling noticeably, as a new larua fresh and hungry, floated up from the ground. "Miles! Oh gods, I saved him!" Tears burned my cheeks. "I saved him!" I wasn't sure why I kept saying it, as if the words would make it true again somehow—I just couldn't seem to help myself. "I saved him. I saved him."

Kiernan shook me. "Quiet. The only reason why I sent you to that maze was to collect him to begin with. When the time comes, I'll return him to his former self so he can be your ticket out of Somniare."

"You stole from my mind, didn't you? The holes in my memory from your … *your minions*, you made them take things from me, didn't you?"

Ignoring my question, Kiernan tightened his grip on me as I continued to fight him, thrashing wildly. The back of my head hit into his nose several times but he didn't so much as flinch. "You've been searching for a human dreamer, and I found one for you. Let you bond with him so he'd be agreeable to taking you with him. I gave you what you wanted."

"At what price?"

"One that you would never have had a problem paying before." He let me go, shoving me forward.

"I've changed my mind, at least about him."

"Would you trade him for Unagi? Because if you don't get to him soon—"

I raised my hands, my magic pooling in my palms. "What does Unagi have to do with Miles? And why did you want me to forget—"

"Stop being so obtuse, *cailleach*!" The wind picked up again, forest debris swirling around us. Voo-Dolly latched onto my leg. "You may not trust me, but trust in me wanting your thanks."

I ground my teeth together, my hands trembling. I didn't know what to believe anymore. "What did you take? From my mind?"

He chuckled. "Ah, that. That has nothing to do with our bargain, but mine with someone else entirely."

"What? Someone bargained for my memories?"

"Yes."

"Who are you? Who are you really?"

The wind halted abruptly, leaves and branches plummeting to the ground. Kiernan laughed as he threw his hood back, his ice eyes dancing with mirth. "I'm surprised you haven't figured it out yet."

I dropped my hands, shifting out of my attack stance. "Yeah, well, maybe it's the holes in my mind."

Arms outstretched, gold light curled from his palms. The swirls of magic formed a picture in front of us, so real it was like standing in the middle of it.

Thirteen witches, both male and female hovered around a large bed, attention riveted to the occupant of the wooden monstrosity. In the center, utterly still, and pale as a ghost, was the witch from the last scene Kiernan had shown me, the one who'd been impregnated by the fae king.

A female wearing a blood-red robe, with hair to match, shifted forward, her head swiveling around to eye her companions. "What about the baby?"

The language rune on the back of my neck burned, translating for me.

"Let it die," someone muttered.

An elderly witch gripped the edge of the black silk sheets, her voice low but confident, "No, we have to save it. This is Elena's child, or doesn't that matter any longer?"

They all began to speak simultaneously, their voices raised with agitation.

"We have no idea what kind of magic it will possess."

"We have to at least see the child before ending its life."

"It'll be an abomination, end it before it ends us."

"Don't be daft, it could be an asset."

"Elena was dear to all of us, and we can't turn our back on her child."

"Silence!" A female I recognized raised her hands, commanding the attention of the room. It took me a moment to place her, but when I did, I stood straighter, the entire scene more important all of a sudden. For she was Agatha Novem, the first Grand Witch of Domus Novem.

"Holy crap, they have to be the original thirteen Grand Witches," I blurted.

Long before I was even a gleam in my parent's eyes, there had been thirteen houses of magic, and peace had existed between all of them. To witness them all there in one place, and all because of this baby I'd never heard anything about until Kiernan had told me was ... odd. Why had I never learned about any of this in my history lessons? Who was this witch that had been so important to all domos magicae? Why had her and her child's history been buried?

"We will remove the baby, and reassess when we've at least laid our naked eyes on it. We owe that much to her."

The other twelve witches murmured their agreement. I couldn't help but grin at how Agatha Novem commanded such complete respect from all the other Grand Witches. There was no one in existence today who could do such a thing. Of course, none of the remaining nine houses could stand to be in the same room. Even though I'd never personally experienced any battles, being from a grey house, I'd never known peace in my lifetime. It saddened me to know how much our magical community had lost.

Agatha glided forward, her expression fierce. "Who will assist me?"

Two witches—one male and one female—flanked her, and the three of them set to work, magic thickening the air. I let my gaze blur, not wanting to witness all of the gory details of a baby being removed from its mother's womb. Gross.

A few moments later, a baby's cry filled the room.

My eyes widened as I got a good look at the child. "Oh, gods." I clutched my throat. "Kiernan."

The image dissolved, and I turned to stare at Kiernan's rigid form. "When you said you were there when the baby was ripped from her womb ..."

"Yes, I was there."

Yeah, obviously. The wail of the baby—him—echoed in my mind. "But how were you there when ... you know, before when your parents—"

"Many things are revealed in dreams." He flipped his hood up, concealing his face from me once more.

"But you said the child was an abomination, and that you didn't know what happened to him."

"I am, and my future is still unknown."

Word games, omissions, but not lies. He was more like his light fae cousins than he knew. "You were the first goblin, weren't you? The first of your kind."

"Correct again."

My mind reeled. If he was the first of his kind— "You should be king. Why are you here? And again I'll ask, what could you possibly need from me?"

"You mean, why am I here in Somniare, feeding some witchling my magic and begging for her thanks? Why aren't I in my rightful place as king of my kind?" A tree cracked and split in half, falling at my feet. The horde of laruas who had been hovering near us swirled up and down, mirroring their master's anger.

"I'll show you why." Magic shot from his palms, forming another scene in front of us.

"Hurry," a cloaked female witch commanded. *"We must finish this before Agatha can find and stop us."*

She moved to the side, revealing a pine box resembling a coffin. But she and her light fae companion were not placing a dead body in it. They were placing a boy, about seventeen or eighteen in it. And not just any boy ...

Kiernan.

Like broken glass, the image shattered before I could see any more.

"That's why I'm in Somniare," Kiernan snarled, his voice guttural. "Because I had to dream myself into existence in this place. And here I've been ever since, while my body lies dormant, frozen by magic, never changing." He pivoted away from me, bowing his head. "It would have been less cruel to kill me."

My heart squeezed, sympathy I never thought possible for a fae of any kind welling up in me. "Why'd they do it?"

"Because I'm an abomination. My powers terrified all of them. All of them except Agatha. And yet they couldn't kill me, for a vow was made. They had to find another way to be rid of me."

I closed my eyes, processing everything I'd just learned. Kiernan had been the first goblin, a race created from the union of a light fae and a witch. He'd been locked away when barely an adult, so obviously he hadn't created any offspring. He may have been the first, but he certainly wasn't the last created from such a union between species. How many witches had lain with fae and hidden their offspring, abandoning them? Enough that an entirely new race had been created—without the help of Kiernan.

And then it hit me, my eyes popping open. "You thought I'd be different because I'm a Novem, like Agatha." He'd just been looking for an ally, someone with compassion. Maybe even a friend. His words came back to me, haunting now that I knew the true reason behind them.

"Would it be so bad to be with someone like me?" One little sentence had spoken volumes, but I just hadn't heard.

"Agatha's the only one who ever gave me a chance, who ever cared." He pivoted on his heel and threw back his hood. "But can you blame them? Look at me! Just look! I don't fit in anywhere!"

I did look. His silver skin glistened in the sun streaming through the trees, his icy eyes piercing me to the core. His muscles rippled with tension. He was devastatingly beautiful, he just didn't, or *couldn't* see it.

"That's not true anymore. There are enough goblins in the world that they're considered—"

"They're all considered abominations. They keep to themselves because they have to. I saw the way you reacted when you realized what I am. And I've seen inside countless minds, all of them think the same. Even my own kind," he spat.

What damage had been done to Kiernan's psyche having grown up the way he did, even before he was imprisoned? And then he'd been trapped in a dream world where the only information he could garner about his kind was from unguarded minds.

I shuffled forward, hesitant, but determined. Kiernan's jaw muscles popped, and he raised his chin, his gaze crackling with pain and malice. But I saw the chinks in his armor. He was wounded and broken, and I knew just what to do … if he'd let me.

He flinched away when I reached for his face, wariness rolling across his visage like thunderclouds. I leaned into him, standing on my tippy toes, forcing my hands onto his cheeks, stroking over his high cheekbones with my thumbs. I pressed my lips on one cheek and then the other, ignoring the way my stomach flipped. "Nothing has changed between us. I hated you for your less-than-stellar personality before I knew what you were. You've lied to me, tricked me, and have generally acted like a grade-A asshat. You want me, or anyone else for that matter, to treat you with anything besides fear and mistrust?" I shoved at his chest, glaring. "Earn it. You don't get to treat everyone like crap and then throw out the goblin card."

His lips twitched. "Goblin card?"

"Yeah, you heard me. Goblin card." I smirked, fluffing my hair. "Now, are you going to stick to the deal and help me save my irksome familiar, or am I going to have to kick your ass?"

"As if you could."

"Hmmm ... I still have a few tricks up my sleeve." And the biggest one was now that I knew what Kiernan's weaknesses were, I could manipulate him.

It looked like I'd finally been dealt a good hand. Just as long as I kept my poker face, I'd have a shot at winning the game.

Chapter 19

Every decision you make, good or bad, rash or plotted out, small or gigantic, are all pieces that form the puzzle of who you are. But if you don't recall each step you took in your life to become who you currently are—are you really the same person? I wasn't exactly sure.

I hadn't wanted to lament the loss of things from my past—didn't want to poke at the holes in my mind, but that was because I hadn't known there was even the slightest possibility I could get my memories back. There was no use crying over spilt brain matter, after all. Knowing that Kiernan had control over the laruas, and could bring Miles back, meant he had to possess the power to return my memories, which changed everything.

"So the part about tracking Unagi wasn't a lie?" I plodded along behind Kiernan through the forest, Voo-Dolly perched on my hip like a small child.

"I do have limitations."

I nibbled on my bottom lip. "Such as?" I was seriously lacking in information about goblins. Sure I knew the general stuff, but I'd never thought to cross paths with one. If I hoped to play Kiernan like I wanted, I needed to make sure I knew everything I could about his powers.

A laugh rumbled in his chest. "As if I would tell you … *cailleach*."

I dug my nails into Voo-Dolly and she shifted, gazing up at my face with curiosity. "If the only creature that ever treated you with kindness was a witch, then why do you insist on using that derogatory term?"

"Because it annoys you."

I ground my teeth together. "I'm fine with it. Doesn't bother me. At. All."

"Right."

I shot the back of his head a death glare and forced my tone to remain nonchalant. "So, what else have you been keeping from me? Since we have the time, care to share?"

"No."

My blood boiled, anger rising within me. *Keep calm. Keep cool. Throwing a temper tantrum isn't going to get you anywhere.* I glanced over my shoulder at the lone larua, the one that used to be Miles. My skin crawled, and my chest ached. "There has to be another human we can use besides Miles."

"My patience for you to find and connect with a human dreamer has worn thin. You couldn't get the job done, so I did it for you."

"But I actually like Miles!" Magic danced along my fingertips, causing Voo-Dolly to yelp.

Kiernan halted, his shoulders rising and falling with his ragged breaths. "We all have to make sacrifices, not that you would know anything about that."

My skin felt too tight, like it was a few sizes too small all of a sudden, and my heart pounded against my ear drums. Images of Unagi, Miles, and even my sister rolled through my mind. A deluge of emotions, too strong for me to single out, threatened to drown me. My teeth snapped into my tongue, the taste of rusted copper dripping down my throat. It was like I was grasping at threads, trying to figure out how to escape Kiernan, Somniare … everything.

Trapped. Trapped. Trapped.

Me naked and tied to Kiernan's bed, siphoning his magic from the ropes that he'd used to bind me, flashed into my mind. *Why hadn't I considered that before? It was so obvious.*

I dropped Voo-Dolly, and she scurried to hide behind one of the trees, sensing I was about to do something either royally asinine or amazingly brilliant. I widened my stance and threw my arms up in the air. "Come to me!" Goose bumps erupted, moving in quick succession across my flesh.

Kiernan whirled around, his expression thunderous. "You dare?"

I smirked, meeting his gaze head-on. "Come to me!" I yanked on his power, the air around us crackling with electricity. The scent of his wild magic burned my nostrils as it surged into me, filling me to the brim. All the hairs on my body stood on end, and I rose off the ground.

"This is a joke," Kiernan snarled. "You can't overpower me. You know what I am."

Despite his denial, his magic continued to stream into me, lifting me higher and higher into the air. I laughed, drunk on the power. "Come to me!"

There was an answering tug—Kiernan attempting to retract from me what was rightfully his—but the scales had already been tipped. It was like trying to scoop the sands of time back into the top of the hourglass when they continued to pour into the bottom.

"Stop her!"

Laruas swarmed me, bouncing off an invisible bubble of Kiernan's magic. What was once his was all mine, including the ability to control the dark creatures.

I gritted my teeth, everything around me suddenly too bright, my skin too sensitive. I plummeted to the ground, curling into a ball. I lay there, my raspy breathing the only thing I could hear.

Minutes, or maybe hours later, my heart slowed, beating its normal staccato rhythm, and my chest rose and fell evenly. I cautiously uncurled, lifting my head to take in Kiernan's crumpled form. I clawed at the ground, the smell of dirt and grass wafting up my nose. I was panting heavily by the time I reached the fallen goblin, and I reached out a shaky hand to touch his perfect features, sliding my fingers gingerly over his smooth skin.

No power flickered through him, his magical light dim, and he wasn't breathing. I leaned in to study him, almost sad at what I'd had to do. It wasn't his fault he'd become the way he was—all trickery and deceit— someone I couldn't trust to help me. But I wasn't going to be a casualty of someone else's mistakes that they'd made centuries ago. Maybe by killing Kiernan I'd actually done him a kindness. Besides, stealing Kiernan's powers—sucking him dry to the point of death—was something he should have expected from a *cailleach* like me.

His body flickered, like an image cast on a wall by candlelight. I pressed my lips against his ear and whispered, "Thank you." His body, nothing more than a ghostly replica of his former self, shimmered, and was snuffed out abruptly. I lurched forward, landing with my face where his had been a moment ago.

Pain lanced my skull, like someone was shooting me in the back of the head at point-blank range, repeatedly. I clutched at my temples and screamed.

"Mama!" Voo-Dolly's voice seemed miles away. "Mama!"

"Rems, please. We talked about this." Unagi's voice swam by my ears.

My reply was close on its heels. "Yeah, I know, but I never said I agreed or accepted it."

I was hurtled into the past … into my lost memories. Some pieces slid into place in my mind, the knowledge of things just there, like they'd never been gone. But the last day I'd lived before coming to Somniare played slowly, as if it was happening all over again.

R.

I LAY ON MY BACK, the white gauzy canopy above my bed rustling from the spinning ceiling fan. I'd just been having the most delicious dream, and I wanted to sink back into the fantasy, to get lost in something I wanted so badly but couldn't have.

"Rems, come on. Time to get up."

I blinked a few times, yawned, and rolled over, breathing in the flowery fabric softener my sheets had been washed in. "Too early. Don't wanna." I wiggled farther into my bed, trying to burrow into the down.

My bed shifted, and hot breath tickled my cheek. "Come on, Rems. You know we have so much to do to get ready for your big night."

I inhaled, the spicy scent of Makoto inciting my senses. My arm popped out of the covers of its own volition, wrapping around the male version of my familiar. His muscles tensed as I tugged him into bed with me. "I won't come out, but you should come in." I rolled over so I was straddling him, his white hair splayed out across my pillow, and his black and white kimono parted to reveal his smooth chest. I sucked in a shuddering breath as I studied a face I knew almost as well as my own.

Slithering my hand inside his kimono, I slid my fingertips over his warm flesh and hard abs, but he snatched my wrist before I could go any farther. "Rems, please. We talked about this."

I bowed into him, touching my nose to his. "Yeah, I know, but I never said I agreed or accepted it." I nipped at him, smirking when I felt his heartbeat speed up. "You don't mean it. Not really."

"I'm not going to mate. It's not like—"

"You want me for your mate, you're just afraid."

"And it's against the rules."

I snorted, snaking out of his grip. "Since when have either one of us ever cared about the rules? Besides, soon I'll be able to make my own."

He rolled me over, holding my hands over my head so they couldn't wander his body. "Rems, don't ruin this day. I—"

"You what?" I arched my back, pressing into him as I dragged my teeth over his nipple.

He let go and jumped off the bed as if I'd electrocuted him. Averting his eyes, he straightened his kimono, covering his chest completely. "It's not natural."

"Please," I huffed. "Don't give me that crap again. I'm bi-sexual, and you're—bi-gender—perfect fit as far as I'm concerned. Plus," I rose to my knees and crawled across the bed towards him, "I love you. Tell me you don't love me."

His eyelids drooped as he watched me, before closing altogether. "You know I love you, Rems. But—"

"Tell me you don't want me. Tell me both of your sides don't want me."

Tension filled the air as Makoto backed up a few steps. "You know all of me wants you," his voice cracked. "So desperately it hurts."

My throat closed off and my chest tightened. "Then why won't you just take me? Be with me? Love me?" I hated how I sounded, so needy, and as desperate as Makoto claimed to be. My kitsune was the only one who ever saw me like this ... vulnerable. I could be myself with Makoto, which was part of why I loved my familiar more than I should.

He shook his head slowly, flicking his gaze around the room. "You're not bi-sexual, Rems. You never—"

I barked out a laugh. "Really? You're going to start trying to define my sexuality? You? Yeah, so maybe the only female I've ever had sexual thoughts about is your female half, but so what? I haven't had fantasies about other males either." I wrapped my arms around my middle, attempting to suppress my trembling. "All it tells me is that I want you, all of you. I want to share myself with you—all of me blending with all of you. And if I'm not truly bi-sexual, who cares? I still want to be with both halves of *you*."

"Rems—"

I steamrolled ahead, just wanting to make him understand—force him to see things my way. "You're it for me, Makoto. Don't you see? I'll forever compare every living soul to you for all of time ... because your soul is what I love. Not what you look like or how you make my body feel. Even though you're so stunning you take my breath away. And every time you touch me I think I could die happy after living that one moment of intimacy with you. I'm selfish, I want all of it—all of you for myself. Male, female ... any way I can get it as long as it's you. You're perfection to me on every level. Why can't you see that? Don't you know? I'd do anything for you. Anything."

Tears pricked my eyes as I waited, gaze averted, for him to react. My lungs burned with each raspy breath I sucked into my dry throat, time dragging to a standstill. *Why hasn't he done anything yet?* I peeked up from underneath my lashes to see him staring at me, the internal battle waging within his eyes. My lower lip quivered. "Makoto ..."

I inhaled sharply as his arms slid around me, surrounding me in the warm cocoon of his body. "I'll be with you forever. I'll never leave you. The bond we have, it goes beyond me and you. We're ... I ..." His fingers dug into my back. "We can't have that kind of relationship, Rems. It's impossible. But you know I'll never mate with anyone else either." I choked back a sob, and he pressed his chin into the top of my head. "I should have been more careful with you. I should have hidden my feelings better. You're hurting because of me, and I'm sorry."

"You're the only friend I've ever had." *And I want you to be the only lover—the only person to ever be in my heart like that.*

"We grew up together, Rems. Our bond is different than any other witch and familiar out there. I'm the only kitsune who ever let themselves be put into servitude of any kind—"

"Because you don't really belong to me. We belong to each other. I branded you, but you knew, even then, years ago, that things were different with us. Our relationship evolving was inevitable."

His warm lips skimmed my forehead. "From day one when I saw you—when I was just a lost pup, alone in the world—both sides of me yearned to have you for mine. As a lifelong companion. If I would have known how much our relationship would eventually hurt you—I would have never approached you."

I fisted my hands in his kimono, pulling. "I wouldn't have survived without you."

"It's me who wouldn't have survived without you."

I APPLIED MY MAKEUP SLOWLY, staring at my bloodshot eyes. The vibrant colors adorning my face, especially the dark smoky shadow and liner helped to conceal the fact that I'd been crying most of the day. *Tonight is supposed to be my big night.* And yet there I sat, alone in my room, utterly devastated.

Makoto had refused to budge—refused *me*. I hurled a brush at my reflection, hating myself more than I usually did. Why had I thought I'd be able to change my kitsune's mind? In a daze, I fluffed my normally straight hair that I'd taken the time to curl. My sable locks cascaded down my back—not that I really cared. *Or, maybe I should.* Maybe I could make Makoto jealous, entice my familiar by flirting with males *and* females from some of the other domos that were attending my ceremony and party afterwards.

Picking up a tube of blood-red lipstick, I spread it across my full lips with care. I stood, admiring the full effect. *Yes, I'll make Makoto so jealous that he'll be fighting himself for who will take my virginity first, his male or female side.*

"Remy, you look beautiful." My mom glided up to stand behind me, a sapphire dress molded to her impressive curves, and a mask to match covering her dainty features.

"Thanks, Mo—"

A sharp jab in my side doubled me over, and my mother's arm slid around my waist, holding me up. "I'm sorry, Remy. So sorry," she rasped against my ear. And then I dropped to the ground, the dagger plunging into me several more times before her heels clicking on the hardwood floor signaled her retreat.

I reached for my magic, but something was hampering it. I coughed, blood bubbling into my mouth, and dripping from the corners of my lips.

Somniare. If I can just get to Somniare.

Everything slipped away.

Chapter 20

Back in the present, in Somniare, tears streamed down my cheeks, dripping into my ears and hair. Why did my own mother murder me? There had to be a reason. She knew I could send myself to Somniare, and told me to keep my ability a secret. There was much more to the story. *There just has to be.*

And why did Makoto have my memories of our past stolen? No, that wasn't exactly right. They hadn't just been stolen, they'd been altered to fit the missing pieces, otherwise, I'd have questioned too much. As it was, I was pushing to have things answered that Makoto couldn't or didn't want to.

Gods, I hadn't known my kitsune—hadn't trusted any part of my old friend when faced with a seemingly new familiar. *Why? Why? Why?* I'd thought getting the holes filled back in my mind would answer all of my questions, but instead, it only brought up more. Two people who I should have been able to trust completely betrayed me. There had to be reasons—maybe even reasons I could understand.

All this time, even though I had no conscious memories of any of it, my subconscious had known about my mother, kept trying to tell me. And my heart never let go of my feelings for Makoto. Even though I couldn't remember our past, I'd yearned for that same connection between us, and was still pushing for what had already been denied me.

I thought about Makoto, being tortured and held by Jared. Could I leave my kitsune there and forget about him? *The betrayal deserves some kind of punishment.* Death wouldn't come to him. Kitsunes were nearly impossible to kill unless you knew how to do it.

I dug my nails into my palms, remembering his laugh, and then hers. Both sides of Makoto, the male and female, dazzled me. There was no way I could ever forget—ever leave my familiar behind. *I love Makoto, every part of that damn kitsune.* I was simply angry and wanting to lash out. I wanted Makoto to suffer … in theory, but I didn't want the reality of it.

I stood, dusting myself off. *I guess I'll just have to take my anger out on Jared. And maybe slap Makoto around a bit when I see him—or her. Doesn't matter, it's all the same to me.*

"Mama?" Voo-Dolly peeked out from her hiding place behind a tree. "You scared me. I thought you were going to take my life away."

I stared at the raggedy doll, something I had created to

comfort myself without even realizing it. Voo-Dolly was not a gift from my sister and therefore held no real sentimental value, and yet … I still wanted my doll. I dropped to my knees and opened my arms. "I won't take your life away, I promise." She ran into my arms, as always, eager for my affection. "Your life is yours to decide what to do with from now on."

Setting her back on the ground, I patted her on the head. Her stitched-on mouth stretched into a grin. "I choose to help you find Unagi."

"My familiar's name is no longer Unagi, it's Makoto, okay?"

She nodded slowly, her expression twisted in thought. "Do I get a new name, too, then?"

"Do you want a new name?"

"Yes, Mama. I want to name myself."

I turned my head and rolled my eyes. Had I made her a bit like Makoto without realizing it? *Probably.* It seemed like everything came back to that damn kitsune, with or without my memories. "Okay, what do you want your new name to be?"

She pulled a pin out of her hand and stabbed it back in. "Mmmm … Eve. Because I'm the first of my kind."

"Eve Novem it is then." I stifled a laugh. She definitely got the ability for naming things from me. *Poor thing.*

I spun in a circle, still drunk on the power I'd stolen from Kiernan. Too bad I hadn't actually learned how to track without being detected. That would have come in handy right about now, big time. That's the thing about magic, just because you possess the innate ability to do something, didn't necessarily mean you could just do any spell.

"So … Eve, think you can figure out which way to Makoto?"

"Yes, Mama. This way." She pointed to the right, waddling into the woods, knowing I was right behind her.

I narrowed my eyes, centering myself.

The time for a reckoning had come.

That stupid warlock is going to learn not to touch what's mine. Because no matter how angry I was at Makoto, that damn kitsune would always belong to me.

R.

MY NERVES WERE FRAYED down to nothing. Our entire trek through the woods in Somniare, a horde of laruas had been hovering behind us, their presence causing the hairs on my body to stand on end, making me hyper-alert. I had no idea if and when Kiernan's power would dissipate. Meaning, since his magic didn't actually belong to me, there was no telling how long I'd have control over it, and by default the laruas. At any moment they could turn on me, changing me into Miles' new shadow companion.

"Go away!" I waved my hands behind me. "Go back to wherever you came from!"

Instead of obeying, they swirled and bobbled around, putting a bit more distance between us and them, but not much. I'd also been trying to figure out how to get Miles back, but that, just like undetected tracking, was beyond my realm of magical knowledge. "I'm sorry, Miles." Hell, I didn't even know which larua he was anymore. They all looked the same to me, nothing more than dark shadowy masses of hunger. *Maybe Somniare did turn out to be hell for him after all. Not that he has any idea at the moment.* What would it be like to not know ... anything? To not feel anything but yearning and hunger?

I tugged at my hair, letting the pinch along my scalp center me again. Something I'd learned years ago: There was no use regretting what was already done. If I could get Miles back, then I would, but I wouldn't obsess about it. Some things are just beyond your control. You didn't have to like the way things turned out, or even forget ... you just had to accept them and move on.

I nibbled on my thumbnail. *"Rems, stop. You're not going to have any nails left soon."* Makoto's female voice floated through my mind, a memory of her scolding me about my bad habit.

I dropped my hand, scowling. "Are you sure you know where you're going?"

"Yes, Mama." Voo-Dolly—I mean Eve bounced excitedly, her pigtails swinging wildly. "We're very close now."

My gaze glided along the forest as we trudged through it. Sun filtered through the trees, forming shapes and patterns, like illuminated clouds on the ground. Birds, colors not found in nature, singing songs with actual words, circled our heads. Somniare wasn't really a bad place, at least when I wasn't falling through magical potholes, getting chased by laruas, being attacked by zombies of varying types, almost becoming lunch for a cannibal baby—I shuddered. Okay, Somniare definitely had more bite than beauty ... quite literally.

"Here! Here! Here!" Eve danced around in a circle, her tiny arms flailing in the air. "This is how you get to Makoto!" She pointed at the ground.

I quirked an eyebrow. "It's a puddle." I stepped closer, peering down at the indentation in the forest floor that was holding about an inch of water at the most. "And a tiny puddle at that."

"It's how you get to Makoto," Eve said, her one stitched-on eye pulled taut, the other gleaming. I think her expression was meant to assure me.

"Okay. How?"

"You go in." She arched over like she was going to dive into a swimming pool.

I fought the urge to laugh. "So it's a puddle portal?"

"Yes." Eve flopped on the ground next to it, passing one burlap hand over the water. "You go in, and come out where Makoto is."

"You sure?" So far Eve had been spot on with her tracking and magic knowledge. But now knowing that my sister hadn't sent her made me question everything Eve claimed to know. I mean, if I brought her to life, wasn't her knowledge coming from me? And I faked my way through most things in life. *Please don't let her have gotten that from me, too.*

"All right. So what, I just step into it?" I eyed the muddy water, crinkling my nose.

"Yes."

"Okay, here goes."

I jumped into the puddle, expecting to sink through or simply appear elsewhere, but instead, I found myself freefalling through empty space. I tumbled end over end, my stomach rising into my throat with how quickly I was spinning. Around me was a tunnel made of dirt, or a hole really—a hole in the earth. It was difficult to make it out with how fast I was plummeting.

I plopped down in a pit of mud. The thick sludge oozed up my nose and stuck to my lashes, covering pretty much every inch of me. Sputtering, I sat up. I was alone. *Looks like Eve has chosen to help find Makoto but not go with me into battle. Can't say that I blame her.*

I staggered to my feet, the mud sucking at my clothes and dripping down my bare legs. After swiping at my face, I spat, the gritty flavor on my tongue making me want to gag. "Now what?" I muttered.

I turned slowly, trying to get my bearings. There were several tunnels leading out from the center of the mud pit, but I had no indication of which one to take. I heaved a heavy sigh and pulled on magic. I didn't want to waste any energy, especially when I was going to need every bit I could get going up against Jared, but I really didn't have a choice. I wasn't about to wander around in the muddy underworld of Somniare while Makoto suffered somewhere.

"Find Makoto," I commanded the small light dancing in my palm. It flitted off, bouncing against the ceiling, walls, and floor, before buzzing down one of the tunnels. It was kind of like following a drunk sprite, or at least that's what Makoto always claimed.

I ambled after the light, sloshing awkwardly in the mud before I finally gained enough traction to pick up speed. I lost my guide a few times, and it doubled back to get me, seeming annoyed, which I knew wasn't possible because it wasn't actually alive. I hoped. It wouldn't have been the first time I accidentally animated something.

Huffing and puffing, I arrived at an iron door that looked utterly out of place in the dank and dark tunnels. It was pristine, not a speck of dirt on it. In fact, I could see my reflection in it, not that I wanted to. I looked like the creature from the muddy lagoon. The light pinged against the door a few times and then bounced at my hand, absorbing back into my body.

Guess this is it.

Sucking in a few calming breaths, I pulled all the spare magic I had to the surface, readying it to explode at a moment's notice.

Then I yanked the door open.

Chapter 21

I'm not sure what I expected, but what I found behind the door, wasn't it. A well-lit, unguarded hallway, lined with more doors is what greeted me. Each door appeared to be made of the same shiny metal as the one I'd just opened. The floor was made of black and white checkered tiles, and each step I took left a muddy footprint, which quickly disappeared.

Hmmm ... Looks like someone has a thing for cleanliness. Wait until he gets a load of me. I laughed, the sound echoing ominously.

I recalled the guide light and set it free, slipping and sliding down the hallway after it. The scent of sulfur assaulted my nose, which meant it had to be ridiculously strong for me to smell it over my own ... earthy stench.

My light bounced against one of the doors on the right before popping out of existence instead of reabsorbing into me. I grunted in annoyance, hating to lose even that little bit of magic, which was why I'd thought to have the go-around by reusing it. Panic shot through me, causing my breath to catch in my throat at the thought of what it could mean. I turned my focus inward for a moment, doing a systems analysis of mine and Kiernan's magic. My heart was galloping even after I assured myself that everything was still where I wanted it to be. There was no way I'd be able to face Jared without the bonus of what I'd stolen from Kiernan since I could burn all of it and not end up permanently dead.

I reached for the door, and—

"Well, well, well. I've been wondering when you'd show up."

I spun on my heel, magic already lighting up my palms. A few feet away stood Jared, his face still obscured by a cloaking spell, his voice the only indication of who he was. "I'm here for my familiar. Hand him over."

He tilted his head, studying me. "Now where did all *that* magic come from? Stole it, did you? Seems we have a lot in common."

"I have nothing in common with a traitorous warlock," I spat. Warlocks lived for power, their entire existence taken up with the need to find more no matter where they got it from—even if it meant murdering their entire domos magicae. It's how one of the original thirteen houses was wiped off the face of the earth.

"You killed for power. I beg to differ."

"No, I killed to save the life of my familiar." *And maybe even a human.* I let more of Kiernan's magic run along the surface of my skin, blue flames rising up my arms, the feel of them cool instead of hot. "Where is Makoto?"

The air warmed around me, laruas rising through the checkered floor. "I don't have time for games with a child," Jared said, his tone bored.

So he could control them, too? I'd wondered about that. "Stop," I commanded, my chest burning with tension. "Suck his memories dry." The laruas spun and whirled, conflicted on who to obey.

"I said to suck him dry!" Fire shot through my veins, exploding from my palms, and skittering along every inch of my skin. Mud dropped to the floor, singed.

Jared screamed when the laruas latched onto him, lifting him off the ground. I smiled, eager for him to become one of the shadowy masses of chaos.

But I should have known it wouldn't be that easy.

The laruas recoiled from Jared when electricity crackled around him. He slumped to the ground, his cloaking spell wavering. Sprinting forward, I blasted him with blue flame, but he raised his hand at the last second, blocking my attack with a shield of water.

Damnit! I have more power than him with what I took from Kiernan but I don't know how to use it properly. The magic Kiernan had been feeding me was nothing compared to what I was now wielding, plus only when gifted can magic truly blend with your own. That was one of the reasons warlocks were always searching for more power—they rarely could hold on to what was stolen. The truly gifted manipulator found a way to con his victims or just plain out blackmailed them.

Jared pulled himself to his feet, his cloaking spell settling back into place, which was not a good sign. He straightened his robes and cracked his neck. "Like I said ... a child."

Water poured over me, slamming me into the ground and dousing my flames. *Child ... really?* Rage suffused my system, burning through my veins and boiling my blood. *I'll show you a child.* Blue flame burst from every pore, surrounding me. The scent of wild magic filled the air, both calming and inciting me. I rose off the ground, my toes dragging across the black and white tiles as I glided forward.

My arms shot out, touching Jared's cool skin as I forced my flames into his body. He grabbed my throat, his fingers tightening in an effort to strangle me. I laughed. He was no match for me, just an insignificant bug that needed squished underneath my heel.

Jared dropped like a sack of stones, his pain so intense that his screams were silent. Even as the cloaking spell dissipated, I didn't get a good look at his features because his flesh was already blackened and melting from his bones.

I turned before his last breath rattled his blackened lungs, knowing there'd be no coming back for him. Some things were even beyond magic.

One with the flames, I blasted through the door on my right, gliding inside. My teeth ground together, and fury churned in my gut. If Jared wasn't already dead, I'd kill him again, and twice as slow. In the corner, on the floor, like discarded trash, was Makoto in female form, blood caking her face and kimono.

I blinked and I was beside her on my knees. "Makoto," I whispered, skimming my fingers over her face.

Her lavender eyes fluttered open, widening when they focused on my face. "You shouldn't have come." Her eyes squeezed back shut. "And you called me Makoto."

"I remember everything." I slid my arms under her, cradling her to me. She hissed in pain. "Shhh ... I'm going to make it all better, okay? I'm going to fix you." Tears pricked my eyes. If only I'd gotten there sooner. I dipped my head and kissed her forehead tenderly, her flowery scent overpowered by the pungent aroma of blood and sweat.

I imagined the blue flames sliding into and around her body without pain, like they did for me, all the while commanding them to heal her. *Please, please, heal Makoto. Heal all of her—heart, mind, body, and soul.* The room glowed a vibrant blue, brightening to the point where I couldn't see a thing. The hum of magic was audible, crackling through the air.

Makoto screamed, and I cried out in tandem, fear that I was hurting her sucking all the oxygen from my lungs. My nostrils flared as I struggled to breathe—struggled to pull the flames back into me and away from her.

Searing pain pierced my skull as a sound akin to thunder rolled through the room. I was flung to the ceiling, where I hovered a moment, the light around me going out. I dropped like a stone, strong arms catching me before I could slam into the ground.

"I got you, Rems. I got you."

Everything went dark.

R.

"WHAT HAPPENED?" I groaned. Someone was doing a tap dance on my skull, I was sure of it.

"You saved me," Makoto said, his masculine voice a low rumble.

I peeled my eyelids open, each one feeling like it had picked up an extra fifty pounds somewhere. Makoto stared down at me, his lavender eyes shimmering with gold around the edges. I struggled to lift my arm, but it too seemingly had picked up some extra weight. Finally, after three attempts, I managed to stroke my fingertips along Makoto's temple and trailed them down his jaw. "You're okay." Now that my memories were back, he wasn't just a pretty face that drew my attraction. He was … home. He was *my* home. I could see it there, inside his eyes—the connection. Our bond was made up of friendship, hard-earned trust, and that intangible thing so few souls ever experienced.

I forced a frown, my lips fighting it. I wanted to throw myself at him, to drown in his scent, to lose myself in the feel of his arms around me. I wanted to forget everything but him, and then I wanted to do the same thing all over again with the other half of him, his female side.

"I think you have a lot of explaining to do," he said.

"Yeah, I suppose I do." I attempted to push myself up, and swayed. I was as weak as a newborn kitten, Kiernan's magic no longer supercharging me. "Looks like I used up all of Kiernan's powers."

"Yeah, I had to heal you after you healed me." He pressed his firm lips to my forehead, his hot breath warming me as he lingered against my skin. "Don't ever do something that stupid again."

I laughed, my head thumping. "This is me we're talking about." I tugged on one of the braids in his hair. "You have some explaining to do, too. More than me."

He gently set me down, his arms sliding out from under me slowly, as if he didn't want to let me go. He then stood, his long strides eating up the room as he paced. "If you remember everything then you know the fight we had that last day."

"Yeah." I intertwined my fingers, squeezing, resisting the urge to reach out to him. "I remember all of it."

"I don't want you to think I had your memories of us erased because … because—" His shoulders slumped. "You don't know what it was like finding you there, so close to death I thought I'd lost you forever. I pushed you away! I pushed you away," he barked out a humorless laugh, "and then only when you were lying there, did I realize how much of an idiot I'd been. I realized that I didn't want to love you all the way so it wouldn't matter if you were taken away. And then you were—taken away."

My heart squeezed. Sometimes I forgot how damaged my kitsune was, having lost all of his family when he was just a pup. Of course he'd have some kind of abandonment issues. "But what does that have to do with Kiernan, and Somniare ... and all of it?"

Makoto expelled a long breath and leaned into the wall, his voice muffled. "I-I bargained for your life. With Kiernan. I would have done anything—anything in that moment when I was standing over your broken and bloody body. You were too far gone for my magic or for Tarik's. Too far." He shook his head as if trying to dispel the memory.

I pushed up on my elbows. "You're still not making any sense."

"I sacrificed one of my tails so Kiernan could use its magic. He went back in time in Somniare and began feeding you his magic as a child so you could send yourself here. I had to buy you time so I could save your life. For payment, he wanted your thanks." He fisted his hands, slamming them against the wall, and growled under his breath. "He wouldn't tell me what he wanted the thanks for, and in the moment I didn't care. I would have done anything to save you. And so I agreed, as long as he took your memories of me."

"But why? Why would you do that?"

"It was my fault what happened. You were nearly dead because of me. You—"

"No, that's not true. You weren't even—"

"Listen to me!" Makoto snarled. "It was my fault! If I hadn't rejected you—if we wouldn't have had that fight—you wouldn't have been alone. I would have been there to protect you."

My lips parted in shock. *What? He blames himself?* "No. It wasn't your fault. None of it."

"And so I thought that me being erased from your memories would make it possible for us to move forward. I thought—"

"You realized you'd made a mistake by rejecting me, but then you had yourself erased from my mind?" I shook my head slowly. "You were punishing yourself."

Makoto groaned. "I should have left you—that would have been the ultimate punishment for what I let happen, but I couldn't. I couldn't leave you." His fingers curled and he scratched his nails down the wall. "And then I thought I would just be your familiar—as if I could keep my distance from you."

"Some part of me remembered you, despite the holes in my mind."

"Your soul remembered mine. I underestimated—no, I cheapened what we had. As if … as if it would all be that simple. Like I could save your life and have the kind of relationship that a witch and familiar are supposed to." Makoto pushed off the wall, his gaze snagging mine. "Nothing has ever or ever will be simple between us, and we'll never be just witch and familiar. I finally accept that."

My heart quadrupled in time, my breaths coming in

shallow little bursts. Was he saying what I thought he was saying? And yet, I was still angry at him. I turned my head, shattering the moment. It was true, my heart and soul had remembered Makoto, and those parts of me had wanted to punish my kitsune even then. It was why I'd felt anger, yearning, and a bit of spitefulness towards him, even though I hadn't been able to figure out the reasons for those emotions.

I rubbed my temples, considering the rest. The whole 'Kiernan time traveling back in Somniare to feed me his magic as a child so I could send myself there when I was murdered' thing was confusing. None of it made sense. And what had he been planning to cash in on for my thanks? "So you were working with Kiernan to force my hand. You wanted me to give him thanks."

"Yes, and no. It was part of the bargain, and I had no choice. But the longer we were around Kiernan, the more I questioned his motives. I was afraid for you. I didn't realize how much control he had of Somniare—and everything else. I'd been grasping at straws, going off rumors of a being that I thought could help me save you. But when faced with the reality of it—of him—I was stuck between a rock and a hard place."

"Which is why Kiernan tried to get you out of the way."

"Exactly. He couldn't kill me, that wouldn't have gone over well with you. But," he pressed his fingers into his eyes, rubbing, "the whole thing back-fired in my face."

He could say that again. "I still don't understand the

time travel element. In order for you to have sent him back in time—"

"Linear time doesn't have to make sense when it comes to magic. You know this. Don't think about it or it will hurt your head."

"Too late," I muttered. Time travel, although obviously possible, was not something most magical creatures messed with for that very reason. Things were entirely too complicated and too much could go wrong.

"And why were you pushing so much in the beginning, about who murdered me, and about everything else? You were—"

"You're not stupid, Rems. I had to be as convincing as possible. Even then you were still suspicious." He pinched his nose. "But I'm not a damn actor, and I kept forgetting what you should know and shouldn't. It was the hardest thing I ever had to do. All of it."

Makoto started pacing again. He prowled past me four or five times before dropping down beside me, taking me in his arms. "I don't know how you did it, but somehow we got around the payment. Now we just have to get out of here and everything will be fine." He pressed kiss after kiss to the top of my head. "It'll all be fine."

"You gave up a tail for me?" It was still taking me time to process everything Makoto was telling me. "But I thought—"

"Anything. I would do anything for you. Which was another reason I had me erased from your memories, it's too dangerous for us to have this kind of relationship. We could still end up like the witch and his werewolf." He clutched me tighter, my cheek crushed against his chest. "But I love you. I love you with everything I am. And I never thought I'd get to tell you that again. So it's too late —too late for distance. I know that now."

"I love you," I whispered, the words escaping from me against my will. Because that was the thing about loving someone ... you could be angry, feel as if you want to kill them even, but deep down you know you can never walk away. Love binds for all eternity. And if you can walk away, it wasn't real love, at least not the soul-deep kind.

I pulled out of my kitsune's grasp, swallowing around the lump in my throat. "We've wasted enough time here. Just because Jared's dead doesn't mean it's time to lounge around and chat. We're not safe as long as we're in Somniare."

I stood, staring down the line of my body. *Leave it to me to have a reunion when I look like I bathed in dirt.* "You tried to hide yourself from me by being the fox all the time, or other forms altogether. And you're being your male self more because female Makoto couldn't handle all the lies. That side of you is too emotional."

"Females don't compartmentalize as well as males."

No one understood male and female energy quite like a kitsune. Makoto had explained to me once that even though his heart and brain were the same at all times, when he became his male or female self, it was like taking out the right tool for the job. He was colored by the energy of each side, his choices and emotions dramatically different depending on who he was at the time. I would never truly understand what that felt like, but it made sense. Sometimes it was just easier to think of them as two different people, although I knew they weren't. Growing up with a kitsune definitely made me view genders ... oddly. It was more about balance instead of competition, which humans seemed to enjoy so much in the modern world. And when my kitsune was the fox, that was the only time he was truly balanced, and asexual in a way.

I shifted from foot to foot, glancing nervously at the door. We'd found a five-minute pocket of peace, the time necessary to relatively sort things out between us, but it wasn't safe to lounge around anywhere in Somniare. No matter how much I just wanted to take a break ... from everything. I was emotionally exhausted, but I didn't have time to really process things just yet. "I hope you know the way out of here because my little guide light is pooped out."

Makoto snorted. "You mean your little drunk sprite light? You never did get that magic right. The more difficult stuff, no problem, but—"

I punched him in the shoulder. "You can shut up now."

I tried not to smile, afraid to jinx us. We might have won the battle, but the war was far from over.

Chapter 22

I paused at the door, tilting my head. "Did you hear that?"

"What?"

"I don't know, I thought I heard something scraping along the floor out there." I pressed my ear to the door. *Nothing.* "Probably just my imagination." I wasn't sure I believed that, though. After all, in Somniare it wasn't *my* imagination we had to worry about.

The door blasted open, throwing me backwards, my body slamming into the wall. Makoto was in front of me in an instant, Tarik glowing white in his hand. I groaned, and reached around the back of my head, my hand coming away with blood. I blinked away the spots in front of my eyes, my gaze focusing in on—

"Aw, come on. I did it, didn't I? I actually walked away before I was one-hundred-percent sure you were dead.

It's like I never saw a horror movie before." I glared at Jared's hidden features. "Such an amateur move."

"Rems, did you—"

"Don't finish that comment, because, yeah, I actually did hit my head."

"That's not what I was going to say," Makoto growled under his breath.

"Enough," Jared commanded. "It seems that Jared underestimated you—both of you. Too bad for him."

Wait. The voice. The voice was different and— "You're not Jared. But—"

Makoto attacked, Tarik blazing a vibrant indigo. Not-Jared waved his hand, summoning a half dozen creatures, massive with red-hued skin, and pig-like features, who pushed past him to engage Makoto. All of them, my kitsune included, moved lightning fast, beyond what my eyes could track without the use of magic.

Not-Jared glided around the melee, bee-lining straight for me. On instinct, my magic rose up within me, causing my palms to heat. "Stay back, or you'll meet with the same fate as Jared."

Not-Jared laughed. "Mmm, you forget, as a warlock I can sense your power levels, and yours are low ... incredibly low. I'm betting you used up everything you could spare taking out dear old Jared."

"How many damn warlocks are hiding out here in Somniare anyways?" I flicked my gaze over to check on Makoto and saw two dead whatever-they-were on the floor. I raised my chin with pride. *My kitsune is seriously badass.*

Metal clanged and beast-like snarls filled the spaces around not-Jared and my conversation, which was oddly civilized, all things considered.

"Did you think that by taking out Jared you had won … whatever this is?" Not-Jared laughed again, the sound causing all of my hairs to stand on end. "Cut off the head of one and another grows back. For we are legion."

"Yeah, well it sounds like your little cult has better things to worry about than us. So we'll just be going now." I pushed myself up, using the wall to keep my balance, my head pulsing in time with my heartbeat.

"Neither of you will be going anywhere."

I flicked my gaze over to Makoto again and counted four dead creatures, and a few random body pieces—arms and hands. I smirked. "We'll see about that."

"You won't be going anywhere." His voice boomed, causing me to cringe.

"Why? Why do you want me? Do you know who I am? Is that why you want me because of that?" Jared's interest in me seemed to be triggered when I'd stumbled upon him in the Somniare winter wonderland. He'd been surprised by my presence at all. Did they know I was the next Domus Novem Grand Witch? Was it about more than just my power? Maybe it was a power play as well?

"We've always known who you are, Aremidalia Novem, next Grand Witch of Domus Novem, and you didn't matter."

Confusion washed over me. "What? I don't—"

"Oh, did you think you were special? That you were targeted because you meant something to us—to anyone? You're just another stupid witch who thinks entirely too much about herself. We just want the delicious power you're holding in you—the one that isn't even yours. Now I want you dead because of the headaches you've caused. Your life means nothing. You are nothing."

"She's special to me!" Makoto plunged Tarik into not-Jared's back, the tip of the katana pushing all the way through the front of his chest.

Not-Jared didn't even flinch. He merely waved his hand, and Tarik disappeared. "Jared was unprepared. I am not." Tarik reappeared in his hand, glowing a sickly yellow with black around the edges. "Thanks for the new toy." He spun, slashing at Makoto, who stumbled back when blood bloomed on his arm.

"No!" I screamed, running and jumping on not-Jared's back. I wrapped my legs around his waist, squeezing, and my arms around his throat, twisting and dragging my nails across his skin. *I'll rip your damn throat out with my bare hands!* He flung me off with ease, not bothering to acknowledge my attack, his focus on Makoto. "Leave him alone!" I jumped on his back again, digging my thumbs in where I thought his eyes should be.

I slammed into the ground, the room tilting on its axis, blood dripping down the back of my neck. I registered Makoto grunting in pain, and somehow I managed to get to my feet, launching myself at not-Jared. "I said to leave him alone!"

I hit the ground … yet again, my vision going dark around the edges. I clawed the ground, spurred on by another grunt of pain from Makoto. My hands trembled and my body shook as I inched towards not-Jared. Grabbing his ankle, I bit, snarling like a rabid animal. His foot shot back, landing square in my face. I sputtered, falling back, the tang of copper filling my mouth as blood dribbled down my throat and gushed out of my nose.

"Mama!" My eyes fluttered shut as rough burlap ran over my face, swiping at my blood. "Mama, I choose to give my life for yours."

How—when did she get here? "Eve? No—" I arched up as a jolt of magic entered my system, buzzing through my veins and heating my body. It was just enough to heal me, with a little extra to fight with.

I sat up, just as Eve slumped over my middle, lifeless. My chest constricted, but I didn't have time to think about that now. I turned towards the battle ensuing between Makoto and not-Jared. Makoto was bleeding from several wounds, and really just playing defense. He had no weapons since his had been stolen, and his magic was still too low to be of any use. I didn't—*we* didn't have much time.

Think, think, think.

And then it all became crystal clear. The one thing that Jared, and not-Jared wanted from me, was the one thing I could still use against the warlock.

Hang in there, Makoto. Help is on the way. Even though my injuries were healed, the blood that had poured from the multiple wounds still hadn't dried. I closed my eyes, searching for the tiny part of me Kiernan had created, the part that knew how to use blood magic.

It glowed like a smoldering ember, deep, deep down, yearning to be stoked into a flame. The magic wanted to be used, wanted to help, and was willing to share knowledge as long as I let it do its will. Symbols popped into my mind's eye, and I drew them on the ground with my blood as fast as I could. When I was finished, I slapped my hand in the middle, giving the mental command to activate in a language I didn't understand, and my rune couldn't even translate, but I still somehow knew how to pronounce.

Time stopped all around me—Makoto and not-Jared frozen in place. My breath stuttered in my chest as a black shadow rose from the center of the last blood symbol drawn, forming into the shape of a large male. Eyes the color of lit cigarettes turned to gaze at me before spinning towards not-Jared. Shadow hands caught him by the throat from behind and snapped his neck like it was a dry twig, tossing him aside. He paused in front of Makoto, who was still frozen in place, arms up in a defensive stance.

"Leave the kitsune alone!" I croaked, not wanting to chance it.

The shadow creature turned to regard me. Its dark,

inky voice slithered through my mind, *"You owe me a favor now, witch."*

I lifted my chin, meeting its gaze head-on. "No. We made no such bargain. I brought you here to kill the warlock. That's it."

"The bargain was made when you summoned me."

"No. That's not how it works. I—"

"It does not matter if you were aware of the rules. They are a part of the accords. Break the accords and I am free to do with you whatever I wish. Blood magic always comes with a price."

Goose bumps patched across my skin. "And what are the parameters for the favor?"

"Learn the accords." The shadow male oozed back into the blood symbol, the air cooling in his absence.

Time restarted, Makoto moving to dodge not-Jared, who was no longer there. "What—" His astute gaze took in the broken warlock in the corner, and me sitting amid blood symbols on the ground. "Oh gods, Rems, what did you do?"

I snatched up Eve, who was nothing more than a doll now, pressing my face into her overstuffed body. I inhaled her sweet scent before I lifted my head to meet Makoto's gaze. "I did what I had to in order to save us. It was the only way." Tears pricked my eyes, but I refused to let them fall. "We need to get out of here. Now. Before we get to meet the next warlock in charge."

Makoto's jaw muscles popped as he ground his teeth together. "We need to wipe away these symbols. Quickly."

He used the edge of his kimono sleeve to smudge them enough so they were indiscernible.

I watched him in a daze. "I guess I wasn't getting out of Somniare in one piece without owing someone or something a favor." I grabbed his arm, running my fingers over his already healing wound. "Are you okay? And what about Tarik?"

"I'm fine, and Tarik will be soon, too. I don't know what kind of magic that warlock used to steal him from me, but it was definitely against Tarik's will. He didn't cut me as deeply as he could have. He fought the pull as much as he could. He just needs time to ... fix things."

"Eve gave her life for me."

"She couldn't have come with us into the real world, you know that, right? At least it was her choice. It would have been worse to leave her behind."

"I hate Somniare. Once we get out of here, I'm never coming back." I stumbled to my feet, Makoto catching me by my elbow. His fingers slid down my arm and intertwined with mine. "To think I used to enjoy playing in this stupid dream realm. Ha! Never again."

Makoto pulled me into his side, his firm lips pressing against my temple. "It'll be okay, Rems."

I shoved at him, hating that he knew how fragile I was feeling at the moment. "Whatever. Let's go." I stormed out of the small room, dragging Makoto with me, my emotions a mass of swirling dark clouds.

Chapter 23

"What are those things?" Out in the hallway, several of the large red, pig-men milled around, their expressions blank and not registering my or Makoto's presence.

"I can't spare the magic to scan them right now," Makoto muttered, his gaze following one of the creatures as it turned and walked right into the wall. "But if I had to guess, I'd say they were created by the warlocks, and without one here to command them, they …" He waved a hand at the one trying to walk through the wall, squeals of annoyance erupting from it as it kept smashing its face in the same spot.

"These warlocks," I glanced over my shoulder, paranoia riding me hard, "did you learn anything about them while you were here?"

Makoto let go of my hand, tugging at both braids in his hair, his lavender eyes glazing over and turning black.

"No. There wasn't much chitter-chatter going on between us."

I let the topic drop, picking up the pace to keep up with Makoto's longer strides. If and when my kitsune wanted to talk about it, I'd be there. I knew a thing or two about repressing emotions. No matter how hard you tried to lock them away, they eventually would resurface, and usually at the most inconvenient times. "So what's the new plan to get out of Somniare?"

"Let's just get out of here first, we can worry about the rest when we get to that part. One step at a time."

I gnawed at the inside of my cheek, my mind unable to focus. Something we both weren't talking about—the blood magic I'd used to call forth, what I was pretty sure was some kind of demon—a demon that I now owed a favor. And what were these accords it spoke of? Domus Novem didn't dabble in black magic so I'd never learned the rules I was sure tenebris witches learned straight out of the womb. I was screwed. The question was: how screwed?

"We'll figure all of it out." Makoto didn't meet my eyes as he yanked open the metal door, leading back to the mud tunnels.

I grunted, wishing he would get out of my head. I was too tired to close my mind off to him at the moment. "Do you think I can still control the laruas?" I thought of Miles, wishing I could bring him back from his void state.

"I'm not sure we should risk it."

Mud pulled at my tired feet, each step more difficult than the last. "But … Miles."

Makoto was silent a moment, no doubt gleaming the information about what happened with Miles, and our adventures and bonding in the maze … and beyond. He sighed heavily. "I'm sorry, Rems. I'm not sure he's worth the risk."

I nodded, my chest constricting. "Yeah, I know. It's just … I liked him."

Makoto halted, and I nearly ran into his back. He turned slowly, his white hair swirling around him. With his blood and dirt-covered kimono, and his tortured expression, he reminded me of some ancient Japanese warrior, fresh from battle, and I guess he was. "Rems, I'm sorry."

I sucked in a sharp breath as his fingers traced along my jawline, before threading in my tangled hair. "For what?"

"None of this would have happened if I hadn't pushed you away."

"You don't know that."

His full lips twisted into a scowl. He didn't argue with me, but I knew he wasn't convinced. I tilted my head back, exposing my neck, aching for him to kiss me there … or anywhere. It was the worst possible time—I knew that—but a part of me wondered if there'd be a later. Somniare had instilled in me a desperation I'd never known before. Things shifted so quickly, there rarely was a chance to enjoy what was a moment ago. It truly was a place of dreaming, where everything slipped through your grasp when you tried to think about it too hard, like when you first awoke from a long sleep, your nocturnal adventures shifting quickly to nothing more than hazy memories ... and then nothing at all.

"I love you, Makoto. All of you. And nothing—nothing will ever change that." My words told him what I hoped he already knew. It didn't matter how angry I was, or what he thought he'd done. Nothing would ever turn me away from my kitsune. Nothing.

My eyes fluttered shut as his lips pressed to the center of my neck, air escaping his nostrils, tickling me. His tongue snaked out, tasting my skin, and then slid up along my jaw, where he nipped at my earlobe. I fisted my hands at my sides, wanting him to have control, but craving it in part myself.

"I love you, Rems. And I'll never push you away again." His hot breath skittered along my cheek, warming me, and eliciting goose bumps.

"No more secrets between us, please. And no more ..."

He shifted, letting my swaying body mold into his, all coherent thoughts fleeing my mind. He cupped my face between both of his large hands, pressing soft kisses to each eyelid, my nose, and all over my face, as if he wanted to sample every inch of me. By the time he took my lips, I was quivering with nerves and anticipation.

This is it.

This is our first kiss since he finally admitted wanting a relationship beyond just witch and familiar with me.

All the kisses that had come before—the stolen and regretted ones, didn't count. Not anymore. This one ... this one would erase all of those, and would be the first of countless to come.

My stomach somersaulted and I was pretty sure I forgot how to breathe for a moment when his tongue swept into my mouth. I savored the taste of him, memorizing each gentle note that made up his unique, spicy flavor. The meeting of our lips and tongues was more than just a physical expression of our love, it was a promise made by our souls. We would share every part of ourselves on every level, leaving no boundaries or secrets between us. It was both terrifying and humbling to know that love like that could actually belong to me—to us.

Makoto wrenched himself away from me, his eyes glowing gold. "This isn't the time or place," he said, his voice breaking an octave lower than normal. "I mean, how many times have you complained about characters, in one of those human fiction books you love, having intimate moments in places that seemed oddly inconvenient?" He grinned, one of his dimples popping out.

"I obviously had no real-world experience with such things. I'll never criticize again." I snatched at the front of his kimono, determined to continue what we started.

He dodged away, laughing. "I don't intend to roll around in the mud with you, Rems. At least not the first time." He winked, causing my cheeks to flush. "Let's get the hell out of here."

I glanced at the muddy ground and cringed. I hated to

admit it but I might have forgotten where we were for a minute. "Yeah, okay. Lead the way."

We continued to plod along in the mud, the tunnel seeming much longer than when I'd first come through it, but eventually we made it to the large mud pit where I'd been deposited by the puddle portal. I tried not to think about how Eve had helped me find Makoto and was now, not dead, but no more. I wasn't sure which was worse. At least in death, there was ... more. To cease to exist—I shuddered.

"Now what?" Makoto asked, inspecting the pit.

"I'm not sure. This is where I landed after stepping into the puddle portal, I kind of figured it went both ways."

Wind whipped from one of the tunnels, bringing with it the scent of death and decay. And then they came, laruas, too many to count, followed by a couple of the red pig-men.

Makoto moved to stand in front of me, but I pushed him aside. Something inside of me yawned and stretched, reaching out dark tentacles of awareness. I felt no fear as I stared into the gaping maws of the laruas, all of them desperate for what we had ... memories and emotions. For I knew I could control them. It wasn't about using magic to overpower them. It was about reaching inside the laruas and filling up the vast emptiness which made them what they were. Because that's the thing about being a blank slate, whoever discovers how truly malleable you are, can write whatever they want to make you do their bidding.

I gathered all of the fury I'd been collecting since my stay in Somniare and pushed it in a wave at the laruas. They ate it up, sucking it all down, and spun on the pig-men, needing to vent the rage they were feeling from me. They didn't care what they felt, as long as they got to feel something.

The pig-men squealed, slicing with swords at the shadowy mass that descended upon them. But the laruas passed right through them, sailing back down the tunnel, obviously in search of better prey.

"Guess you were right about them being creations or the laruas would have gobbled them up."

"Rems, we need to go." Makoto picked me up and slung me over his shoulder, pushing off the ground. We rose up into the air, heading straight for the mud ceiling.

"Look out!" I covered my head with my arms on instinct. I should have known to trust my kitsune, though, because we passed right through the ceiling and were immediately tumbling through the air, upwards.

I squeezed my eyes shut, not liking the sensation of falling up. Makoto grabbed my hand, yanking me into him, and wrapped his arms around me so I was under his large body. His lips skimmed my ear. "I got you."

We were spit out of the puddle and landed in a mass of tangled legs and arms in a pile of leaves. I groaned, and lifted my head, hitting my forehead into Makoto's cheek.

"Ow," he muttered. "Watch it."

I stayed where I was while Makoto extricated himself from me, my gaze on the canopy of trees over us. "What a ride, huh? I can't wait for the normal laws of gravity to apply again."

My skin prickled with awareness and I sat up, swinging my gaze around. "Something's coming."

"Yeah, I feel it, too."

The smell of sulfur met my nose first, followed by the crackling sound of fire. The trees around us began to burn, the smoke quickly clogging the air.

"No, it can't be." Makoto stared in disbelief, his eyes shifting to black. "They can't get out unless …" He yanked me to my feet. "Run, Rems. Run faster than you ever have in your life."

My throat constricted. "What about you?"

"I'll be right behind you, I promise. Just don't look back. And don't stop. Whatever you do, don't stop."

A tree branch crashed to the ground, missing us by a foot at most, the flames consuming it heating my legs. "But where am I going? We need to—"

"Go!" He shoved me and I stumbled forward.

If there was one thing I'd learned over the years, it was not to question Makoto when it came to such things, which is what terrified me. If he was as panicked as I thought he was … well, chances were, running wouldn't really do any good.

But I did anyways.

Chapter 24

Love and hate are two sides of the same coin. People usually live for one or the other. It drives them … shapes them. Living for love is a fragile state, though, because if you lose your love—what you're living for—then you no longer have a life. A part of you always knows it, and is terrified—terrified that at any moment you could lose everything.

As I ran across the once green landscape of Somniare, trees, shrubbery, leaves, birds, and other animals all burning around me, I learned the true meaning of terror, the kind that made it hard to breathe. It was wondering if Makoto was still behind me, and not being able to bring myself to look to find out one way or the other. It was like Schrodinger's cat; as long as I didn't look, Makoto could still be fine, and I refused to believe anything else. I refused to acknowledge that I was in that box, too—my life possibly already over and I just didn't know it yet.

When I hadn't remembered Makoto—when all of my memories of us, our relationship had been stripped from me, I'd been reckless. It was because I had nothing to lose. Now, I had everything to lose.

"Aremidalia Novem," the fire hissed. "Come to us. Dance with us. Let us love you."

I pumped my arms harder, kicking my legs higher and faster. What I heard, the flames themselves calling to me, was like nothing I'd ever dealt with before. I sensed the dark magic, the feel of it in the air suffocating, worse than the actual smoke the fires were creating. The voices pressed in on my skull, drowning out the screams of the forest creatures burning alive, which I was almost thankful for.

"Aremidalia Novem, come to us and we will make you part of us." I covered my ears and screamed, stumbling, but still managing to stay on my feet. "Let us love you like we did Makoto. He and she are one with us now. Join us."

"No!" I screeched. "It's a trick! I don't believe you!"

"The kitsune gave itself for you, but you don't want that, to be separated again. Join us. All of us. Let all of us love you."

No! No! No! I refused to believe it. I wouldn't. I would know it, sense it if Makoto was dead. Our bond was too deep for my familiar to be ripped away without me feeling it in my bones. *But what if ... what if I lost— No! But what if* —I tripped over something, the smoke blurring my pathway.

A hand reached for me, snagging around my wrist. A

tremor ran through me from the instant recognition. "Makoto!"

I wasn't sure how he'd gotten in front of me, nor did I care. All that mattered was that he was still alive, and I would keep him that way. "Come on. Lean on me." I slid my arm under him and hoisted him to his feet. His head lolled a bit, finding a resting spot on my shoulder. I lurched forward, his feet working but partially dragging with each step.

"Come on, Makoto! You can do this!" Sweat coated my skin, and my lungs burned, but somehow, with my kitsune by my side, I moved forward.

"Call Tarik. Call for him. Now," Makoto croaked. "He has to be fixed. He has to be."

Tarik! I mentally shouted. *Please, come to me. We've never needed you more.* I felt the buzz of his magic in my hand, but he didn't appear. It was as if he was trying to, but just couldn't manage. "I felt him. But he didn't—"

A string of expletives I'd never heard come out of Makoto's mouth singed my ears. "Fix yourself faster, damn sword!"

I bit my lower lip, grunting under the weight of Makoto. With each step he slumped more into me. "Tarik, please! Hurry!"

The magic hummed in my hand again, but still nothing. The smoke was so thick around us that I couldn't see more than a few inches in front of my face. But at least the flames had stopped speaking to me since I'd found Makoto.

"Rems, I'm sorry. I've been screwing everything up since the beginning. I thought I could save you but instead I'm just going to get you killed twice." His fingers dug into my side painfully. "I'm sorry I wasted all the time we could have had together."

"Stop it," I growled. "Just stop it. This isn't the end. Do you hear me? It's not—" I coughed, my burning lungs swallowing the rest of my words. "This isn't good-bye," I rasped.

My hand jolted with magic, Tarik popping into existence in my grasp. *Oh, thank the gods.* He glowed gold, almost blending in with the flames around us. But no magical armor appeared around me, Tarik still too weak to conjure it. "What do I do with him? How do I fight them?" Without the armor there was a chance I'd be burned.

Makoto slipped from my grasp, tumbling to the ground as Tarik swung my arm, in total control. He yanked me to the right, swiping through flames, sucking them into himself. I was then yanked to the left, Tarik sucking all the flames he touched into him, as if he was feeding from them.

And on it went—me, spinning, spinning, spinning ... until I was a bit dizzy and a lot giddy with Tarik's emotions. The sword was drunk on the power he was eating, and his ego was even larger than normal. I laughed as we tracked down each and every ember, smiting that which wished to smite us. "Take that! Did you really think you were a match for us? Did you? I don't even need armor!"

"Tarik," Makoto admonished from his prone position on the ground, "I need it. You have to share."

Now that the smoke had cleared, I got a good look at Makoto, and my heart shriveled. Most of his hair was gone, what was left covered with soot. His kimono hung from his body, his exposed flesh blackened and bubbled, some patches showing bone.

I can't ... I can't— I clawed at my face with one hand, shuddering, unable to look away.

Tarik glowed pink, and I felt the love he had for Makoto, as much as he hated to admit it. He flew out of my hand, piercing Makoto's chest. I clutched at mine, remembering the feel of Tarik buried deep within my flesh and bone. Golden light bathed Makoto, lifting him off the ground. He cried out, his arms and legs splayed in pain, and a moment later, Tarik disappeared.

Makoto sat up, his gaze saddened. "He's never had to give his life before, and now he's given it twice in Somniare."

"He loves you." I knelt beside him, burying my face in his newly regenerated hair, the scent of burnt flesh lingering. My gut twisted as I forced the image of what he'd looked like mere minutes ago from my mind. *He's fine now. Everything is fine.* "I thought—I was so scared." Makoto was the only creature in existence I would ever admit that to. He was the only one who got to know all of me, weaknesses along with strengths.

"I know."

"What were those things? They weren't really fire, that much I'm sure of."

"Demons. They were demons."

"Real demons?" I squeaked. Unlike what humans thought, demons had nothing to do with God or hell or any place mentioned in any bible or religious papers. Hell was actually a place, where all kinds of creepy crawly species existed. Usually, they were more than happy to stay there, battling amongst themselves and leaving the rest of us magical beings alone. My knowledge of demons pretty much consisted of the 'stay far away from them' variety. Tenebris witches were known for summoning them to do their dirty work, but there was always a price, just like my shadowy visitor had informed me before.

"You don't think this has to do with what I did, do you? The blood magic?"

"I don't know, Rems. Maybe the gate you opened wasn't closed properly. They did seem pretty intent on getting to you specifically."

"No, I owe the other one a favor. The one I summoned, he—"

"You owe him a favor?" Makoto's eyes flashed red, and then black. "What? Why would you—"

"He said it was part of the accords and that it didn't matter if I didn't know. It was part of the payment for summoning him. If I didn't agree then he could do whatever he wanted to me."

Makoto buried his face in his hands, his voice muffled. "This is not good. Not good at all."

I dug my nails into the charred dirt. "What was I supposed to do, let that stupid not-Jared warlock kill you?"

He dropped his hands, glaring at me, his eyes glowing a deep crimson. "You didn't give me a chance. You just jumped right in and made the mess we were in even worse."

"He had Tarik!" I threw a clump of dirt at him, hitting him in the forehead. "You were bleeding!"

"You did not just throw dirt at me," he growled.

"You're being an idiot. Maybe it's time female you came out to play because male you has an ego the size of … of something really gigantic." I fought the urge to stick my tongue out. "He would have killed you and I did what I had to do to save you."

"You're being—"

I pulled myself to my feet, stalking away from my stubborn kitsune. "We don't have time to discuss your ridiculousness. We need to get out of Somniare before Tarik has to sacrifice himself a third time."

Makoto grabbed my arm, spinning me back to face him. "What exactly did the demon you summoned say? Was there a time limit or any kind of …" He fisted his hair and tugged. "Any kind of anything I need to know? This is important."

I locked gazes with Makoto, his features pinched with worry. "I know it's important. I know that. But he didn't say anything else besides the fact that I now owe him a favor. When I attempted to disagree he said either I pay the favor or he can do whatever he wants with me. I figured option number one was better, and then he went back to wherever he came from."

"This is really bad, Rems." His eyes glistened and he flicked his gaze away, as if it pained him to look at me.

Standing on my tiptoes, I softly pressed my lips to his smooth cheek. "Let's not worry about it right now. One catastrophe at a time." I wound my hands through his hair, smiling against his skin. "By the way, why haven't you changed back into female you at all since I rescued you?"

"Rescued me," he mumbled under his breath. "Please."

"Did something happen back there that you—she is having trouble dealing with?"

Makoto slipped away from me, crossing his arms over his chest as his eyes flashed lavender. "The only thing either of us has trouble dealing with is you."

I scowled. "You're no walk in the park either ... *Unagi*."

His face twisted into a scowl to match mine. "I can't believe you named me that."

I giggled. "I can't believe you let me."

A small smile twitched up his lips, as his arms slid around my waist. He dipped his head to whisper in my ear, "I've always been a fool for you."

He pressed a lingering kiss to my forehead before moving away from me. "Now, let's figure out how to get out of Somniare once and for all."

Chapter 25

I kept shooting furtive glances at Makoto, his jaw muscles popping as he ground his teeth together. His gaze had taken on a faraway glazed-over sheen, his thoughts obviously elsewhere.

"So …" I bit at my thumbnail and then dropped it quickly, hoping he hadn't noticed. "Back to three tails now, huh?" I turned to watch a purple bunny munching on what appeared to be a chocolate carrot. *Is someone having an Easter dream?* When I got no response from Makoto, I pressed, trying to make our trek through Somniare a bit more … palpable. The silence between us was killing me. "I remember when you were so pumped to get your fourth one. Will it eventually grow back, or are you at a twelve-tail cap now?"

"I don't know," he mumbled.

"You don't know? Seriously?" I flicked his arm.

"What? Why are you flicking me?"

"Did you even hear what I said about your tail?"

"I think we're going to have to risk you calling the laruas. Or at least the one who used to be Miles. Maybe you can tap into the magic to change him back like Kiernan was going to. Hopefully, it won't use up much energy."

I snorted. "Nope, wasn't listening at all."

"What?" he snapped.

"Nothing," I growled.

He touched my shoulder, his fingers dancing down my arm. I shivered with delight. *Pathetic.* He was using my body against me. How quickly he was willing to turn the manipulative tables on me. I decided to deign him with a response anyways. "I'm willing to give it a try. It's not like we've come across any more human dreamers. Just their dreams."

As if to prove my point, a guy bearing a freaky resemblance to Freddy Kruger burst out of the forest hot on the heels of a wanna-be Michael Meyers. It was almost comical, if they both weren't headed straight for us.

"Run!" Makoto shouted, tugging me into motion.

"We've been doing entirely too much cardio in Somniare. I guess it's a good thing we don't need to eat."

I couldn't decide if it was irony or not that the Freddy Kruger rip-off had shown up in the dreamscape. And what about the wanna-be Michael Meyers? What did he have to do with dear ole Freddy? It seemed like some human was an old-school horror movie fan. Couldn't say that I blamed the dreamer, the old movies were decidedly better when it came to originality. And Johnny Depp had even made an appearance in the first *Nightmare on Elm Street* movie.

How did that song go again? One, two, Freddy's coming for you ...

"Rems, stop thinking about the merits of old horror movies and run faster!" Makoto twined his fingers with mine, pulling.

"I'm perfectly capable of running on my own, thank you. So stop pulling me like I'm a rag doll," I snapped. *Three, four, better lock the door ...*

"Then do it!"

I dramatically pumped my arms faster, glaring. "They're not even that fast. Besides, Freddy's the tricky one. Michael just keeps coming and coming but at a very considerate pace." *Five, six ... five, six ... Damnit!* I always forgot what came after five, six.

I glanced over my shoulder. "Hey! Hey! You, Freddy! Do you know what comes after five, six?"

"Come to, Freddy!" His hideously burned face cracked a smile, his yellow slimy teeth causing me to cringe.

I clucked my tongue. "Seriously? That's all you got? Your dreamer probably knows, so you have to know. The song goes ... One, two, Freddy's coming for you, three, four, better lock the door ... Now what comes after five, six?"

"I'll kill you nice and slow!"

I sighed and rolled my eyes. "He's not going to answer."

"You've lost it, you know that, right?" Makoto hissed,

although his lips twitched into a half smirk. "And it's five, six, grab your crucifix."

I snapped my fingers. "That's right, why do I always forget that one?" *Seven, eight, gonna stay up late. Nine, ten, never sleep again.* Having finished the song in my head, I laughed to myself. *Huh. Maybe I really have lost it.* Too much time in a dream world may do that to … anyone. It could seriously do that to anyone.

Just as sorta-Freddy called out something else threatening at us, wanna-be Michael's theme music swelled, although it wasn't exactly the same rendition as from the movies.

"Do you think the dreamer is one of those scary movie sketch comedy guys? Because Freddy and Michael are slightly off."

Makoto swung around, wielding a purple glowing Tarik. With one smooth arc of his arm, both horror movie icon rip-offs lay in separate pieces, cut through at their waists.

I clapped my hands together, grinning. "Tarik, you healed faster this time!" He glowed pink, popping into my hand as if to say hi, before disappearing.

Makoto frowned. "Sometimes I think he likes you better than me."

Laughing, I patted him on the arm. "Don't be silly. Of course he does, it's me." I spun in a circle with my arms out, more laughter bubbling up within me.

"Rems." Makoto grabbed me, attempting to hold me still.

I tugged away from him to resume my spinning, my laughter taking on a manic edge. "Isn't this place grand? Maybe we should just stay. I mean, it would never get boring. Never. Ever."

"Rems, stop. We have to—"

"Never! Ever!" In the back of my mind, I knew something was wrong with me, but I didn't have control over whatever it was.

Two fairies, the stereotypical kind that didn't actually exist in real life, burst out of the forest, giggling with the same maniacal edge that was leaking from me. Each of them took one of my hands and we began to dance in a circle, my body knowing the steps that my brain didn't. Wings sprouted from my back, stretching for the sky, shimmering in the sunshine as I continued to spin with my new friends.

Makoto grabbed at me, but I slid past him with ease, shooting him a thousand-watt smile. "Let's stay! Let's have fun forever!"

"Yes! Stay with us!" my friends said in unison.

"We'll never have to worry about anything again. We can just dance, and laugh, and have fun forever—"

"And ever!" my friends finished for me.

I threw my head back and laughed. It was the kind of laugh that was carefree, and it felt amazing. I wanted to hold onto the feeling with everything I had. But I also wanted to share it with Makoto.

"Dance with us, Makoto!"

He said something in response but I couldn't make it

out over the dull roar of laughter surrounding me. The day was dazzlingly bright, the birds chirping happily, and even the air I breathed was extra fresh. *I really should just stay here forever. I'd never have to deal with complications again. Who needs them? Life is meant to be happy. Why can't I be happy too? Happy ... forever and ever!*

No. This isn't you. You would never hide in Somniare because your life got a bit difficult. These aren't your thoughts. Fight them. "Happy here forever!" my voicebox forced the words from my mouth even as I continued to wage my internal battle.

I squeezed my eyes shut and stars danced behind my closed lids, urging me on in my crazed jubilation for life in Somniare. Images of Makoto and me together, away from the judgmental scorn of my kind, in complete bliss, filled my head. And I wanted it, so desperately.

But it wouldn't be real.

Who's to decide what's real and what's not? If you believe it, it's real.

No, that's not how reality works.

It does in Somniare.

Yes, it does in Somniare.

"I want something real with you, Rems. I want all of you—the good, the bad, and the ugly. I don't want a Stepford witch. I want you. My imperfect, confusing, infuriating—"

My face contorted as I forced my smile into a frown, the edges of my lips resisting the change. "I'll give you infuriating!" I stumbled out of the circle, snatching my hands away from the tight grips of my fairy friends.

A few feet away, Makoto sat on the ground, cross-legged, his arms resting on his knees, and a smirk tilting one half of his mouth up. "That didn't take as long as I thought it would."

With my newly grown wings I leapt into the air, landing on top of him. "How dare you! I just want to have a perfectly nice life with you and you're just sitting here insulting me?"

He rolled me over, his weight pressing me into the ground. "I don't want nice with you, Rems. Nice is boring. I want it all. I want to experience everything there is to experience with you by my side."

I stared up at my familiar, my kitsune, my best friend, and the love of my life. His eyes swirled with laughter, love, and the kind of understanding that only came around once in a lifetime. His soul understood mine, and mine his. "You might want to pick your words more carefully next time."

He chuckled. "I did."

My eyes widened, and I twisted around to where I'd been dancing with the fairies, discovering they were gone. "Wh-what happened?" I shook my head, trying to rattle my thoughts back into place. "I felt … crazed. Happy, but crazed."

Makoto stood, helping me to my feet. I rolled my shoulders, the wings gone. "Those were a different brand of demon. Worse than the first in a way."

My mouth swung open. "Those were demons?"

"You were too caught up in the black magic to feel it."

I shuddered as I thought about how deliriously happy I'd been. That was more dangerous than the flames which had tried to consume us. Using false happiness to control someone was easier than threatening, and most of the time the victim had no idea they should fight, let alone want to. Plus, it's a lot creepier somehow. "Why weren't you sucked in by them with me?"

He shrugged. "Not sure. Maybe because they got to you first and I saw how it affected you."

"Yeah, I guess." Or maybe I was the one being targeted by the demons because that's the way it seemed to me. "Why all the demons all of a sudden? You can't tell me it's a coincidence."

"No, I don't think it is. We need to get out of here fast before we run into any more of them."

I stared into the dark recesses of the woods, everything a bit too quiet for my liking. "If the next round of demons is already here, it could be anything."

Makoto slung his arm around my shoulder, his breath warming the top of my head as he pressed a kiss there, lingering. "So we make our next move immediately. Which is to call the laruas. If we can return Miles to his former self, then you can ride with him out of here."

My gut twisted. I wanted to return Miles to … Miles, but I didn't want to steal his life. He wasn't just a faceless human anymore. I liked him. Cared even. And as odd as it sounded, the moment I'd gotten my memories of Makoto back, I hadn't wanted to steal a human life because of him. Makoto wasn't like me. He—and she—all of my kitsune was good, pure even. Yes, despite my familiar's influence, I still made a lot of shady choices, but over time I found myself wanting to be better for, and because of Makoto.

"I'm not sure I could do it—take Miles' life."

Makoto stilled, his muscles tensing. "I get it, I do. And normally I'd be overjoyed with you feeling that way, but—"

I slumped into his chest. "But I might not have a choice. Him or me, huh?"

"Yeah. I'm sorry, Rems."

I snorted. "It's fine. I may want to spare him, but we both know I'll never be that selfless. I want to live. And I'll do what I need to do to get my life back."

Makoto tightened his arm around me, both of us pausing to revel in the feel of the other, knowing that the worst wasn't behind us yet, but looming in the road right in front of us.

Soon we'd find out if we really would have a future together, or if our fates were meant for a much darker path.

Chapter 26

"Concentrate, Rems," Makoto's female voice chastised.

"I am."

I forced my eyes shut, blotting out the image of my newly transformed kitsune. Makoto thought it best to be the female side in order to help me meditate. Before changing, he'd claimed that his male side was feeling much too volatile and a female touch was needed in order to bring calm and order to the situation. I thought it was a bunch of crap. For all the understanding Makoto claimed to have over male and female energies, things were put in a box too neatly sometimes. Males could be calming, and females volatile, I was a prime example of the latter. I was pretty sure kitsunes were sexist, as weird as that sounded. I mean, how can someone be sexist if they can check both boxes? But it was true. There was entirely too much gender stereotyping going on when it came to Makoto's opinion on things.

I dug my nails into the dirt, inhaling and exhaling slowly a few times before pushing myself up into a sitting position. "I lied. I can't concentrate. My mind is ... completely unfocused."

Makoto's soft pink lips parted, flashing perfect white teeth. "I know."

"You don't have to be so smug about it." I crossed my arms over my chest.

"Not smug, I just know you." She trailed a finger down my arm, clearly meaning to be affectionate, but eliciting a different reaction from me. Goose bumps erupted across my flesh.

"That's not really helping." I pivoted forward, capturing her arms and falling back with her under me. Nuzzling her neck, I inhaled her more feminine scent before sucking on her thumping pulse. "Bet you thought you'd have more control in this form." I laughed. "And you probably do, over yourself, but not over me."

"Rems," she whimpered as I kissed along her jaw, "we can't do this now. No matter how much I want to." Her back arched, pressing her body into mine, her soft curves tantalizing, making me want to trace every one with my tongue.

"Mmm ..." I cupped her face, forcing her lips to part so I could ravage her mouth. She welcomed me, despite her protests, and I lost myself in her, our kiss deepening with each passing moment.

A flash of her bloody and bruised body skittered across my mind, forcing me to think of all the things we'd both been through recently. *She's right. We can't do this now. It's not the time or place.*

I rolled away from her, my chest heaving. I forced my gaze away from her flushed face, and reddened lips, grinding my teeth together. "Who's to say we're going to have much time for these kinds of things when we get back to the real world? I was murdered, things are going to be different."

"We can make the time there. Here, things are less under our control."

I nodded, swallowing around the glass shards in my throat. Closing my eyes, I forced myself to relax, turning my concentration inward. *Show me how to call and free Miles. Show me.* My body buzzed with awareness as my magic jostled within my system as if I was being shaken, the black magic attempting to rise to the top. *Show me.*

My hands had the urge to move, and without opening my eyes, I let them. A bitter taste bloomed on my tongue just before all the air in my lungs was sucked from me.

A dark, inky voice slithered through my mind. *"Another favor. That's two now. Be careful, witch, or I'll own you soon."*

I was falling, my stomach somersaulting as I gasped for air, my eyes tethered shut.

And then I was in the forest in Somniare, the same place I'd been before, not having moved an inch, Makoto and everything else around me frozen in time.

The smoke demon with the ends of lit cigarettes for

eyes hovered in the air above me, and the distinct impression he was smiling was impressed upon me, even though it had no distinguishable features.

I forced my lips to move, to speak the words I needed even though my head was spinning. "I don't owe you another favor. I didn't call you this time."

"You did call, whether you made the conscious effort or not. You want this larua," he waved his hand at the black swirling creature behind him, *"to be returned to the form of the human boy. You asked for help to do so. I came."*

"No, I asked—"

"Whether I perform the task or not, you still owe me a favor for calling me."

"This is a godsdamn racket! I didn't call you!" He hovered, burning eyes strained on me as he waited. "Fine. Bring Miles back."

"I thought you'd say that."

"Did you come for Kiernan, did he owe you favors, too?"

His laugh rolled across my mind, chilling me. *"One does not play such games with Kiernan. You, on the other hand ..."*

The demon disappeared in a puff of smoke. When I blinked, time restarted all around me, and Miles stood several feet away, a dazed expression on his face.

"What happened?" Miles muttered, rubbing his temples.

Makoto whipped her head around. "You did it."

"No." I gnawed on the inside of my cheek. "It wasn't me."

Somewhere deep inside panic was taking hold. I was just too tired to really feel it … yet. By having Kiernan feed me his magic, I was tainted by the dark, I was a tenebris witch whether I'd chosen that path or not. It may have been made worse when I stole what wasn't freely given, but in the end, I was changed by the deal Makoto made with Kiernan.

And even though Kiernan hadn't been forced to bargain with demons for whatever reason, I'd opened a door that I didn't know how to shut. *I'll just have to never use any black magic again.* But that wasn't going to fix the fact that I already owed the smoke demon two favors. What if he forced me to use more black magic, and therefore I ended up garnering more debt? What if demons were nothing more than black magic loan sharks, and there was no getting out once you were in?

"Hey, it'll be okay." Makoto squeezed my hand, her eyes searching mine. I'd closed off my mind from her, not wanting to tell her about the second favor. There was no point in both of us freaking out about it. I knew she'd think I was merely saddened by my need to kill Miles, which was true, too.

"Yeah." I let her fingers slip away, turning to give Miles a forced smile. "What do you remember?"

He straightened his glasses on his nose, his eyes glazed over. "I remember those things. They … I—" He wrapped his arms around his middle, shuddering. "And then nothing." He dropped to the side to lean against a tree.

"But I can't shake the feeling that—I don't know—I was lost. I felt lost, but—I can't describe it."

I brought my thumb up, nibbling. "You were one of the lost, so that makes sense—the larua. But you're fine now."

Makoto slapped my hand away from my mouth. "Stop biting your nails. I thought you broke that habit."

I scowled. "I've been under a lot of stress lately."

"Not an excuse."

"Of course it is!"

"Are you two really arguing about nail biting right now?" Miles' face was incredulous. "Is it a chick thing?"

"I can't believe you just said that!" I threw my hands up in the air. "And to think I liked you."

Miles grinned, all boyish charm. "I was just kidding."

"Mmm hmm …" I rolled my eyes. Funny how people always said they were kidding when they got a bad reaction from the intended audience.

"I can't believe I need to say this again," Makoto grabbed my shoulder and spun me around, pointing in the distance, "but … Run!"

I swore under my breath, more annoyed than anything else. Marching towards us, led by another not-Jared I presumed, was at least twenty of those red pig-men creatures. "Looks like they're ready for round three."

"What are those things?" Miles squeaked as he ran past us.

I sprinted after him, Makoto beside me. "Doesn't matter, you're having the right reaction. Now which way?"

"What?" he snapped.

"The door out of here, remember? Which way?"

"Ummm …" He hung a lefty, plowing through a bush. Several angry bunnies gnashed their abnormally sharp teeth at him.

A flash of purple blazed in my peripheral and I glanced over to see my kitsune in fox form, tails whirling. I smiled. It meant Makoto's powers were almost back to normal.

"This way! The pull is getting stronger!" Miles yelled.

I glanced over my shoulder, the not-Jared and goons not rushing after us, just going slow and steady. Guess they believed in the adage: slow and steady wins the race. Personally, I was all about a need for speed when it came to most things.

The three of us rounded a bend, and I stumbled, rolling down a hill. The scent of grass and dirt exploded around me, and I cringed when I smacked into Miles, who had obviously taken the same tumble.

"Is that it?" Makoto's multi-layered fox voice demanded. "Is that what we're looking for?"

Miles crawled forward on his knees, reaching a hand out in awe. A hole had been ripped into the very fabric of Somniare. Inside pulsed the night sky, twinkling with all the light of multiple galaxies. Each way out of Somniare was personal, and somehow this one fit Miles perfectly. He was infinite possibilities, just like outer space seemed to be. *And I'm going to take that all away from him.*

"Yeah, I … yeah, it is. I can feel it."

I shook my head, feeling Makoto's eyes on me. "I can't do it," I whispered.

"You have to."

"So how do we do this? How do I bring you with me?" Miles asked, his gaze still riveted on his doorway.

Tears pricked the corners of my eyes. "You take my hand and we step through together."

He turned to face me, his expression soft. "I know what's going to happen."

"Yeah, I told you. We—"

"It's okay. I don't mind giving my life for yours. I just want out of here. Maybe I'll find peace wherever I'm going."

I blinked rapidly. "H-how did you know?"

"I just did when I came back into myself. I'm not sure how, but all of the information was in my head." He reached out his hand, offering it to me. "I think maybe I always knew. Why else would someone like you take an interest in someone like me?"

"No— I mean, yes, that was true at first, but you're … I genuinely like you, Miles. I really do." Tears spilled down my cheeks. "I'd never spent time with a human before, and if they're all like you, I have to say, I've misjudged your race."

He snorted. "They're not all like me." His eyes clouded over. "My stepdad certainly wasn't."

"I hate to rush this," Makoto interjected. "But—"

"What about you? You'll be right behind me, yeah?"

My fox nodded. "I can use dreamers' doors, but I can't

open them myself. And being that I'm not half dead, or pseudo-alive, I can leave any time I want as long as the door is open."

Miles took my hand, and we stood, both of us staring into the dazzling scenery before us. "It really is beautiful." Miles squeezed my hand, and I glanced up to see that he was looking at me now.

Rising onto my tiptoes, I pressed my lips to his. "Thank you."

"So that's the secret to getting thanks from you. One has to stand on the precipice of death for you to utter those words. Of course, I found that out the hard way." Kiernan's lilting accent stiffened my entire body.

"No. I killed you."

"I'm not that easy to off, *cailleach*."

Squeezing Miles' hand tighter, I shifted so I could see behind me. Kiernan stood with feet wide apart, hood thrown back, and his icy blue eyes swirling. "I did what I had to do."

"As do I." He grabbed Makoto, my fox yelping as it tried to escape Kiernan. "I will call upon your favor now."

I nodded, my entire body numb. *If I just agree then he'll let Makoto go.* "Tell me quickly. We're about to have company."

Kiernan laughed. "Them? They're all dead. It'll take some time before a new warlock steps in to lead."

I gulped. "Okay."

"You will find and free me in the real world."

Freedom—a chance at a real life. I should have known.

But at what cost for the rest of us? Kiernan would be the king of the goblins, more powerful than even I could imagine. But ... he commanded me to find and free him, there was no time limit. I could play in the grey just like I always did.

A knowing smile spread across Kiernan's face. "I won't waste your or my time laying out all the parameters for the conditions, I know how that would work with a *cailleach* such as you. I can see your wheels turning even now." He chuckled. "No, too much effort and in the end there would be no guarantee I'd get what I wanted. So instead, I'll motivate you to complete the task as quickly as possible."

He ran a leather-clad hand through Makoto's soft fur, pausing over the protruding ribcage. "I'll be keeping this," he plunged his hand into Makoto, ripping out my fox's beating heart, "until you fulfill your duty to me."

"No!" I screeched, dropping Miles' hand. "No!"

Makoto slumped to the ground, crimson smeared across the once pristine white fur. Kiernan waved his hand, the wound closing even though Makoto's beating heart was still resting in his open palm.

"Stop," he commanded. "Or I'll kill your kitsune now."

I sputtered, and dropped to my knees, not knowing how he wasn't doing that now. "Please ..."

"A kitsune can live without its heart, at least one of them, but the longer it goes without it, the more it ... changes. After a while, the poor creature will never be the same." He pushed a booted foot against Makoto, causing me to whimper. "This one has already given up so much for you. Don't make it suffer anymore."

I watched numbly as he tucked Makoto's heart into a leather pouch attached to his belt. "Now, go."

As if he was being controlled by Kiernan, Miles yanked me up, intertwined his fingers with mine, and jumped through the door. I didn't bother to fight as I was pulled with him, but I couldn't tear my eyes away from the scene I was leaving behind.

Grinning at me, Kiernan picked up Makoto's prone fox body, and hurled it into the door after us.

I'll do whatever it takes to save Makoto, but when I'm done ...

I will make you pay Kiernan. I swear it.

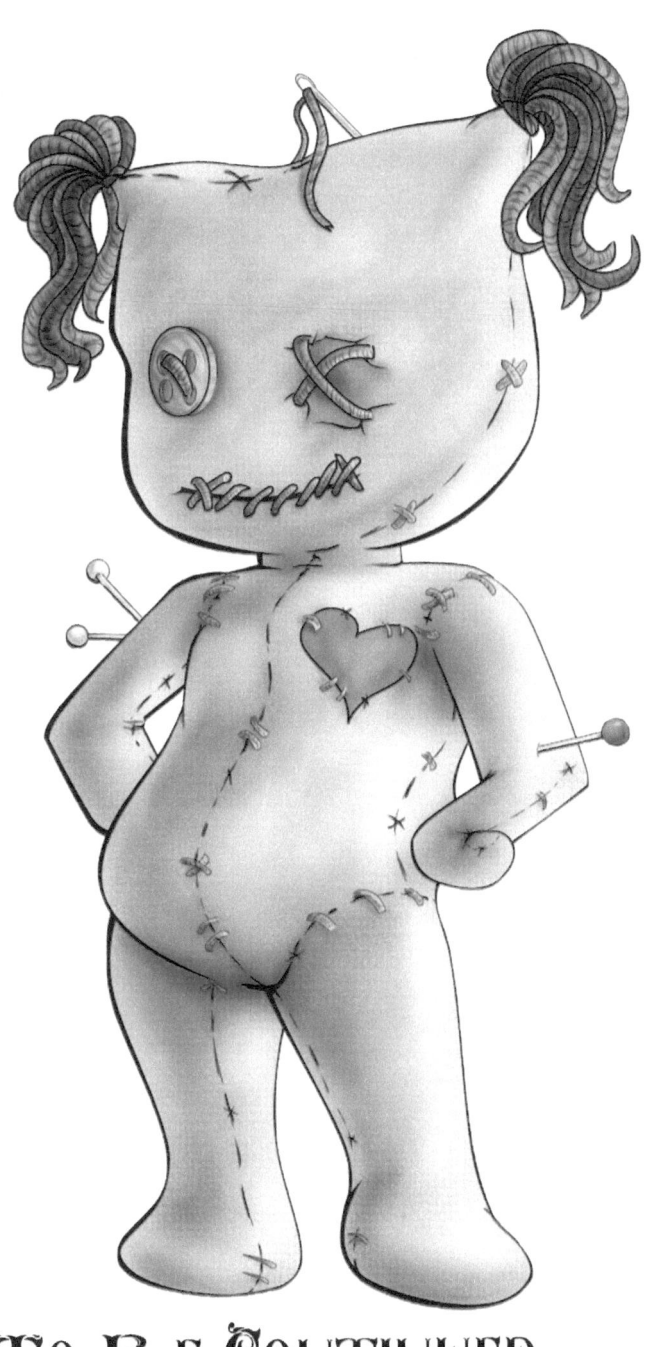

TO BE CONTINUED...

Acknowledgments

As an overthinker, acknowledgments are quite an arduous task for me. I wonder if I'm being lackluster or too intense with the thanks. Or did I forget someone? Possibly I gave too much credit to someone and therefore slighted someone else who actually did a ton. A part of me doesn't want to include these in my books at all because the people I appreciate should know it already ... or do they??? No matter how I look at it these damn acknowledgments make me friggin' sweat.

But here they are anyways since if I don't include them then people will probably think I'm ungrateful and weird. I mean, I am weird, but I don't want people to think that. I am grateful though, so I'll just go-ahead and make this uncomfortable for everyone. Heh.

Okay, here I go. Right now. Actual acknowledgments to follow. Hopefully, they represent an appropriate level of gratitude to all the people in my life that deserve it.

(And yep ... I have totally copy & pasted what comes next from my *Replayed* book acknowledgments, which I originally took from *Virtual Reality Bites* acknowledgments. I thought maybe after *Replayed* that I'd come up with something better. Or at least something new. Obviously not. So this is now copy & paste edition #8. Or 9? 10? Who even knows anymore. Therefore, I'm thinking you should probably get used to it.)

My amazing Hubby! Words can't begin to explain how supportive and truly amazing he is. Hmmm … I think I already used the word amazing. But unlike in books, when honestly applied to someone, the word amazing means something, well, amazing. And my hubby is all of the things that word implies. Romance heroes are nothing compared to him.

Lindsay Tiry … what would I do without you? I hope I never have to find out. From cover design to interior graphics to logos, you do it all. Your talent is awe-inspiring, and I hope one day everyone else will be able to appreciate how you shine.

Melissa Ringsted … my illustrious editor. Without you, this book probably would have gone straight into the trash. Thank you for giving me the confidence to publish when I convinced myself that I was the worst writer in the history of writers, and for fixing all the words.

Ren, Kristin, Shona, Ruty … my O.G. chicas … I wouldn't be here without you. I'm beyond lucky to know all of you.

And last, but certainly not least, thank you to everyone who has taken the time to read this book. Hopefully, you enjoyed it, but even if you didn't, I still appreciate the fact that with so many options out there today, you even gave my book a fleeting chance.

About the Author

Ava Wixx escaped into books at a young age and decided to stay there. It was only a matter of time before she was driven to create her own fantasy worlds from fear of running out of places to explore.

Reader, writer, dreamer ... Ava only toils in reality when absolutely necessary. She lives in North Carolina with her husband, and spoiled mini-poodle.